RAVAGING MYTHS
By
Frederick Marshall Brown

Copyright 2009 Frederick Marshall Brown
Published by P450Guide.com
ISBN 0-97000-843-0

PROLOGUE

Man first occupied the Americas over a hundred thousand years ago and has survived events that led to the extinction of many other creatures on the continents. Destined to wander, he traveled in pursuit of food from other continents around the globe and ended up in the Americas like everywhere else mostly by chance. Over the millennia the influx of people migrated from the outer reaches of the Americas to the interior, slowly populating both continents. The people who eventually crossed the ice age Beringia land bridge were only some of the more recent arrivals in prehistory. Assessing this from the present, each successive wave of people could be viewed as either immigrants or invaders on their arrival in the Americas, and we may never know what their impact was on the inhabitants already present. We do know that many complex and unique cultures developed, flourished, and then disappeared over the course of time leaving mere remnants of their prior existence.

By the time the Europeans crossed the Atlantic and landed in the Americas, millions of native people with thousands of distinct cultures already occupied the two American continents. Unfortunately, the European arrivals had an absolute disregard for the people already present. Even though they were immediately struggling, the new arrivals were determined to claim what they called the 'new' and 'uninhabited' land for their already existing imperialistic countries across the ocean. The Europeans were nothing more than invaders clearly set from the start on taking the Natives' land by any necessary means even to the extent of outright genocide.

Sadly, this is what happened in our own recorded history. But the Americas did not have to evolve in that way. Changes at innumerable points in our history could have led to a tremendously altered world.

The world of Ravaging Myths traveled a different path. The native population was not decimated by European disease. The millions of natives would have fared very differently against 16th century invaders.

2

CHAPTER 1

I arrived.

The smell of hot dogs and stale popcorn filled the otherwise dry, clean air. Only I could smell them, and I hated hot dogs and popcorn.

It was starting over again, and all I could think was 'we make our own hell…we make our own hell…'

It had once been simple.
Wakeup.
Eat.
Go to work.
Work.
Eat.
Work.
Go home.
Eat.
Go to bed.

The pattern fell apart during 'go to work' number whatever, a particularly regrettable weekend day on which I had been covering my friend's patients for him while he was on vacation out of the Shawnee Nation. Cross coverage is a standard practice among physicians, and you do it for others if you ever have hopes of taking vacation yourself. That, or pay through the nose for a locums doctor and have complaints from your patients for months afterwards because let's face it, a temp is a temp. Patients would generally rather have their own doctor, but in their doctor's absence, they preferred a handpicked local colleague over a temp any day. It's reasonable. Opening up the details of your bladder, bowel habits and everything else medical is rough on a person. Throw in some diarrhea and a little STD or some sexual dysfunction and, well you get the picture. Having to cross that 'Hello, this is me and this is my disgusting and embarrassing problem' bridge once in a lifetime with a stranger is already one too many. That aside, I was filling in for my friend and had to take a quick ride to Marion to do hospital rounds on the few patients he had there. This

3

entailed a short drive north up the congested International freeway, and then another short hop to the hospital.

We have to insert "CRASH" at this point. Actually, not just "CRASH", but "CRASH WITH LIFE-THREATENING, COMA-INDUCING, PLATE IN MY SKULL HEAD INJURY".

Everything changed....

It started like this...the smell of hotdogs and stale popcorn...

The accident had been horrific. Thirty-two dead, a hundred and seventeen injured. Fog had been to blame, or at least fog, and a long convoy of eighteen-wheelers. It had been early A.M., and a high-speed traffic stream had been headed up the freeway towards Chicago. Crazy fog lulled us all into a driving stupor. Then, one mistake led to another, and..well, I think the picture has been made pretty clear..

I was one of the lucky ones, not dead, but not really all that alive either. You see, I was in a coma. Peacefulness and bliss under the influence of morphine poured into my veins to sooth my horrifically broken body. Outward appearances could be deceiving, but not in my case. That was as good as it would get for me after that wreck. Or, at least, that was as peaceful as it was going to be for me from then on. Of course, I didn't know this at the time because I was in a coma. Like I said, peacefulness...bliss...

Life sucks, and then you die, but only if you're lucky.

For me, the smell of hotdogs and stale popcorn filled the air.

O.K., here we go...Rhythmic, but uncontrolled 'flopping' (i.e. seizure), and my coma world shifted. The horrid smell of hot dogs and stale popcorn faintly lingered, but nothing else was familiar.

That was what it was like the first time it happened I can theorize, and one of several times I don't really recall because of the coma. Even so, the beginning is always the same now, and I can

4

speculate that it was always the same when I was comatose because it hasn't changed since. At least not until the next painfully fateful day I have to tell you about. This one truly changed everything.

As with me, I suspect that reliving the past is a tremendous nightmare for most people. I doubt that very many people would honestly want to go back and repeat a stretch of their lives without being able to edit as they crawled back through the seconds of that time. Imagine my misery as I recalled and related that brief period in my past to you. Not the best example of a good day in my life, to say the least. Now imagine even the best day of your own life…take the time to imagine that single, wonderful day….and then, fill the spaces left between those very fleeting moments which you actually choose to remember. What do you come up with but another crappy, miserable day that you desperately cling to for the shear sake of preserving your sanity? All in all, as I said, life sucks, if you haven't heard it and actually acknowledged it before now.

My name is Marcus by the way…Marcus Lemonte. Doctor Marcus Lemonte as if anyone particularly cares at this point. Welcome to my own personal hell. And so we begin…

Spring had arrived in the Shawnee Nation, a generally beautiful time in a part of the country which includes virtually every inch of the region between the Sioux Nation to the west, the Cherokee and Chickasaw Nations to the south, and the Iroquois Nation to the north and east. The emergence of the leaves and the green fields could easily hold your attention, if you weren't otherwise occupied with the many cruelties of life. Unfortunately, this cruelty swallows up most people, and few actually acknowledge the good inherent to their environment until they're destined to leave it, i.e. a foot in the grave or more horrendous in some respects, a trip to the Shawnee Nation's epicenter, Chicago. Whatever the case, the Lemontes had no encroaching plans for either. The warm, bright day took them

5

unhesitatingly to one of the region's most beautiful locations, and they were soon scrambling up a steep slope towards Camel Rock.

Camel Rock, so named because it looks very much like a giant stone camel, is one of the Shawnee Nation's many scenic areas, and is swallowed up by the Shawnee Forest that spans the lower portion of the Shawnee Nation. Although Camel Rock is the most prominent feature, because how can you miss a giant camel, the region has many interesting and beautiful rock formations and multiple scenic viewpoints where the countryside can be seen for miles in most directions. Having done the top of the rock thing more times than they could count, the Lemontes started at the base of the hills for a change, and Marcus was soon lost in his own thoughts.

Struggling through the tall grass of the hillside, he felt the uncomfortable sensation of eyes probing his back. He had climbed nearly three hundred feet, but the feeling had not diminished since he first hit the densely overgrown trail. It was becoming unbearable, but he would go on to the top of the hill like a trooper. Nikki wouldn't understand if he suddenly gave up the climb, and he didn't think he would blame her. This insidious paranoia had been slipping in to his life since the crash, and hearing about the eyes boring into his back at the moment would only piss her off, to put it mildly.

Behind him, a small rustling briefly caught his attention, and his heart took a sudden lurch into overdrive with a new surge of adrenaline. His fear and anxiety would have been blatantly apparent to Nikki if she weren't so preoccupied with the very real struggle of maneuvering up the damn hill. The pounding in his chest drove him frantically to within a foot of her back.

"Hey, Nik.. do you want to take a break?" He blurted out in breathless desperation.

But she kept scrambling further up the hill, slipping in the loose rock as if fleeing from his question. She had to have heard him, he thought. He was only a few feet from her.

"NIKKI!" He screamed at the top of his lungs,

6

nearly losing his balance in the process.

With a swish of blond hair, her sweat-drenched face was suddenly glaring back at him. Her eyes blasted him with annoyance as she plopped down among the bug-infested weeds. He began to itch just looking at her slim, grass engulfed form.

"We're almost to the top." She stated matter of factly.

"I...I know." He stuttered, trying to mask his panic. "I just need a second." But he knew she saw through him. She had become very familiar with his wide-eyed paranoia, a little too familiar for his own fleeting comfort.

Suddenly, a multi-legged form the size of a small truck scuttled down his arm, and the sensation sent him into a wild, flailing frenzy. Before he could even begin to get control of himself, he savagely smacked his arms and legs as the crawling seemed to overtake his entire body. The loose earth beneath his feet quickly began to give way and he slid backwards hopelessly. He felt the damn bug insistently driving towards his brain as he struggled to grab hold of any solid and stationary object in his path. But then the grass that had been a struggle to crawl up through gave way like open-air to his crazed attempts to stop his backward slide. Within seconds he plummeted to a rock ledge one hundred feet below Nikki, cracking his skull on the unforgiving stone when he landed. The ledge was a lucky break, if you could call it that, considering how far they had already crept up from the bottom.

His blackout was brief, but still long enough for him to find Nikki's hysterical face hovering over him when he came to. The pain rapidly engulfed his few coherent thoughts as he tried to get a grasp of what had just happened. No good, the pain was too much. He needed to go to sleep if he wanted to escape it. Drowsiness swept in, and he gratefully started to close his eyes. Nikki grabbed him by the shoulders and shook him, shook him hard. His pain multiplied beyond belief! She was trying to kill him as surely as the bugs had been boring toward his brain. With an enormous effort, he forced his eyes open to the blinding

7

sunlight and tried weakly to lift his head.

"Marcus, are you all right?" she begged, tears rolling down her face and fear apparent in her voice even in his dazed and semiconscious state.

"Uhhh.." The sound of his own voice pounded the throbbing melon that had once been his head. "I don't think so.." He forced out before he could be swallowed back up in darkness, the smell of popcorn and hotdogs nauseatingly taking a backseat to the pain.

The sudden onset of trembling in the rock ledge under his head quickly compounded the roaring pain that ate voraciously at his battered brain. The bugs had burrowed in somehow and were doing some massive damage! The violent tremors scared him into opening his eyes again, and he vaguely realized that Nikki was no longer hovering over him, if she ever had been. His pain became so severe that he believed he could literally feel waves of searing agony rushing through his body. The whole world surrounding him vibrated with a horrendous roar that made him feel like death was imminent, and he could clearly taste the rancid hotdogs whose stench filled his nose to the point of suffocation.

In what seemed like an eternity, but could in reality only have been minutes later, a gradual calm claimed the earth and slowed the small avalanche of rocks that had painfully showered Nikki and Marcus. By Shawnee Nation standards, it had been one hell of a quake, a six at least, and unheard of in the area for lifetimes. In fact, the last time this part of the Nations had shaken so hard, reports were that the Mississippi River had actually flown backwards for a while. Any buildings in the surrounding area would have eaten the full force of the quake, but stranded there on the ledge two hundred feet from the base and at what seemed to be the center of the earthen distress, the ability of any local building to take the quake was far from the first thing on Nikki's mind. Marcus was out cold, and judging by the quickly swelling mass on his forehead, he had a concussion at the least. Even though she wasn't formally medically trained herself, the years of

her life she had spent with Marcus had blessed her
with enough superficial knowledge to bring a list
of pretty damn scary thoughts to her head as he lay
there unconscious. She knew it was proof that
sometimes a little bit of knowledge could really be
a bad thing.

Gently lifting his head, she discovered his
hair was completely dry and his head was devoid of
oozing or spurting blood. She tried her best to
scan for any obvious damage, but knowing the names
of injuries and having the ability to find evidence
of their presence were two very different things
and the latter was well beyond her superficial
knowledge. The anguish of uncertainty quickly
filled her mind as the helplessness of her
situation gradually settled in on her. He was the
doctor, damnit, and he couldn't do a damn thing for
himself now! Tears refilled her eyes as their life
together flashed through her thoughts.

Had she not been so distractedly terrified
during the quake, Nikki would have seen Marcus's
eyes roll back into his head and tonic-clonic
movements rattle his body almost in time with the
shaking of the ground. The seizure had been as
brief as the quake, but just as troubling. Marcus
hadn't experienced a full-blown generalized seizure
since waking from the coma after the freeway
tragedy. Up to that point, his foul-smelling auras
had only preceded lapses in awareness that were
extremely short-lived for the most part. Even
then, their frequency had been serious enough to
make him question his own ability to drive on
several occasions since the coma. He was all too
aware of the impact losing his driver's license
would have on his ability to practice medicine as
well as on his life in general, and had
deliberately not followed up with his own
neurologist after leaving the hospital for that
specific reason. Seizure disorders always had to
be reported to the DMV when confirmed, and he
wasn't about to let that happen to him. He was
still in possession of his full mental faculties,
and his driving was generally limited to short hops
from his home to the clinic or to the nearest
hospital most of the time. The wreck had put his

friend permanently in his debt for cross-coverage without any need to reciprocate up until now. He knew it was primarily in response to guilt on his friend's part, but every effort to change his friend's mind had failed.

With a loud groan, Marcus's eyes flickered open to instantly squint at the glaring sun in confusion. Blinking rapidly, he struggled slowly to his elbows, dizziness tempting his eyelids back to rest.

"What the hell!" he muttered in disbelief. "Where am I?"

"Just take it easy, Marcus," Nikki sighed with relief, "you've had a nasty fall and been out of it for awhile..."

Ignoring her attempts to care for him, Marcus tried to clumsily get to his feet. Waves of nausea passed over him as he nearly blacked out a second later, but years of fighting back the same sensations induced on by a deluge of disgusting experiences in medicine remarkably carried him all the way to his feet. The brain-rattling headache that also seemed to make the ground shake beneath him was another story. Ibuprofen wouldn't take care of this one, to say the least.

The thought of another fall scaring the hell out of her, Nikki jumped up and grabbed his arm before he stumbled over the rock ledge in obvious confusion. A major aftershock nearly sent both of them to their knees before she managed to wrangle him to safer ground at the back of the ledge. Marcus swayed in her arms as he kept up a failing effort to fight off sleep. She had to get him down off the hill before something worse happened. Stepping off the relatively safe ledge, she forced his sagging body into a sitting position and pushed him ahead of her as they slid down the hill using the loose rock skittering beneath their bodies as transport. A few nerve-wracking minutes later, they managed to make it to the base of the hill before another aftershock rumbled a ton of stone into a small landslide that traveled the same path. Before the next round of shaking could hit them, she managed to steer Marcus's barely responsive body to her car where she finally pushed him into the back seat with a desperate groan.

"I'm taking you to the hospital, Marcus," She blurted out breathlessly as the engine revved kicking the car harshly onto the road.

Marcus didn't respond... He had been swallowed into the post-ictal darkness of sleep.

The day had begun slowly at Krepp's Corner Market on Main Street in Hawthorne, Shawnee Nation. The days always began slowly there, and the Krepps had no desire to change it. They had taken up the slow life for the best of all reasons. Once a busy psychiatrist in Chicago, Ray's life had been uncontrollably speeding like a locomotive without brakes, or at least it had been until his doctor warned him that his severe heart condition was insidiously taking over and stealing days from his life. He had known about his high blood pressure for several years, but even as a doctor, hadn't taken it seriously until his stress test revealed significant ischemic changes. Even then, he had plowed on until the tightness gripped his chest, sending tendrils of dull pain down his arm and up into his neck like a creeping dread. Several days in the hospital doped up with morphine and subjected to a cardiac cath had changed his perspective. He had to make a life change, or not have a life worth living. The little town of Hawthorne had been the answer, and he had difficulty imagining anyplace better now. With a mostly immigrant population pushing a whopping 3000, and nestled in the depths of the Shawnee Nation Forest, peacefulness and isolation were their only options.

Of course, his wife Hedda had been thrilled with the idea of returning to her old hometown. She had wanted to move back for several years, and his health gave them the best reason they would ever get to make such a dramatic change. Fortunately, they had been preparing for retirement since Ray's first day of work, and they were financially well off, particularly for a town the size of Hawthorne and in the rapidly declining Shawnee Nation. Running the old corner store put them casually to work, introduced them to the people of the town, and gave Hedda something to do to occupy the time she had never been able to adequately fill after their children left home. They couldn't over-do-it, and they would probably lose money with the prices they marked to keep people from traveling off so far for their groceries. The point was, they were together, and Ray was still alive.

The low rumble that caught her ear as the shelves began to rattle brought a memory back from her childhood. She had felt a small quake or two as a girl, but earthquakes were relatively uncommon in the Shawnee Nation, even though the hills of the Shawnee Nation Forest straddled a major fault line in the region. A big one had been predicted a few years back, but its predicted time had come and gone without the rattling of a teacup. As most of the unsecured store shelves wobbled violently and some eventually toppled, she also had trouble staying off the floor. The quake was magnitudes worse than those in her past and about as unexpected as a dead man sitting up in his coffin. In less than a minute, a large portion of the store's contents had tumbled to the floor. The panic she felt in her stomach slowly faded after the vibrations stopped. The old brick building was built to withstand the tests of time. The sirens that were already blaring outside ominously told a different story for other parts of the town. Seconds later, she felt Ray's arms wrap firmly around her from behind, and she knew everything was O.K. for now.

In a nursing home forty-five winding miles from Hawthorne, an eighty-seven year old man was finally succumbing to death. His death was well deserved and would also qualify as overdue in the eyes of most of the people of Hawthorne. The general consensus was that he had kicked the bucket years before, and he had long since slipped from most of their thoughts. The religious fervor that frequently gripped the immigrant town of Hawthorne led to a communal belief that God wouldn't allow

such evil to exist in the world for long. Not so
remarkably, he had often been the focus of
persecution nearing that of the Salem witch-hunts.
His insanity and talk of ghosts and demons in their
midst confirmed their beliefs about him and
strengthened the congregations of more than a few
fundamentalist churches.

Eagan Portraire had moved to Hawthorne in the
late forties to work at the Lemonte Funeral Home.
The town had cautiously accepted him and his
assorted family members initially, but his first
trip to the Center had changed that. Before then,
he had been an isolative, hard-working man who had
respect for but didn't fear the dead. Their
opinions began to change shortly before he was
first sent away. Eagan's unusual activities before
and after his trip to the Center were very
disturbing to the holier than thou residents of
Hawthorne even though the town's people were
initially ignorant of his real problem. Portraire
was rumored to keep strange and unacceptable late
night hours in the funeral home 'performing his
duties'. The town people never understood why the
Lemontes, respected as they were, allowed such
inappropriate behavior to continue on right under
their noses. But it did and was virtually
unhindered for many years except during the times
when Eagan was kept locked up in the Center.

Most of the people who had observed him make
his way across town in the middle of the night
ranting and raving at his unseen traveling
companions learned to travel the streets
exclusively during daylight. They quickly spread
word of him, and whole households would stare from
their darkened windows as he made his way home.
Sometimes they even caught sight of him running
down the street as fast as he could while screaming
incoherently as if he was being chased by the devil
himself. Not a single person ever made an effort
to help him during his time in Hawthorne.

Towards the end of his frequently interrupted
life in Hawthorne, his activities drifted even
further toward the frightening and fantastic as he
began to avidly approach people to warn them of the
demons surrounding them in their otherwise peaceful

13

town. The psychiatrists at the Center continued to attribute this to his chronic paranoid schizophrenia when he was finally readmitted there for the last time around ten years earlier. By then, even the newer medications couldn't touch the well-entrenched delusions that filled his ever-shortening life. He gradually slipped deeper into his own bizarre world as he spent his remaining years wandering the halls of nursing home after nursing home.

But as if he had some mystical insight into the exact time of his death, Eagan Portraire called for the nursing home director on what would be the last day of his life. He claimed to have urgent business that needed to be taken care of immediately after his death, if not sooner.

"Yes, what can we do for you?" the director suspiciously asked as he walked into the room, all too aware of the direction Eagan's thoughts had taken lately.

"You have to deliver this envelope to someone in the town of Hawthorne. You have to do this immediately, or you shall suffer for your incompetence." he shrieked out, as if in his last breath.

"I'll make sure that it's done, Mr. Portraire." The director said somewhat smugly.

Although the threat of violence in a locked nursing home was ever present, no dying person had ever threatened him in such a caustic way. Especially not a patient as lost in the head as this old man always was. He was very aware that Portraire had a long history of mental illness, but an Alzheimer's component must have slipped in during the past few years to push him even farther over the edge. Taking the envelope, the director left the old man to die in his own time. It would probably be pretty soon by the ashen green pallor of his face. Ashen green was not the glow of health and was definitely not something that was easily forgotten. Perhaps a transfer to the local medical hospital was in order. They were generally more than happy to get a hold of the extra dollars, in spite of the potential liability if he died.

When the director entered his otherwise well

14

kept office, he threw the envelope on a pile that
stood three feet tall beside his desk. There were
just too damn many things to do with his workload.
He'd eventually get the envelope to somebody to be
dealt with properly. But it wouldn't be done this
late in the afternoon. It was five PM after all,
and everyone including himself had more important
things to deal with. Besides, he needed to get
home to check his house after the good-sized quake
he had felt earlier in the day. The news had
reported it was centered some sixty miles away, but
you never could tell what would happen to
structures built without regard to the region's
earthquake history. With his luck, his house would
be a pile of rubble and he would have to move back
into one of the rundown hovels on the facility
grounds, again deprived of the distance from the
facility he often needed to maintain his own
sanity.

CHAPTER 2

Having painfully woken in the car shortly
after leaving Camel Rock, Marcus had belligerently
refused to be taken to a hospital. He still
remained somewhat confused, but that only added to
his obstinance and hostility leaving Nikki with no
choice other than to ferry him back home. She
barely managed to get him up to bed before he
collapsed and slept through the remainder of the
day and the entire night, barely moving in his
sleep. Nikki lay next to him anxious and wide
awake for half the night wondering if she had done
the right thing by bringing him home like he
demanded. At the time, she had believed she didn't
have a choice, but now she wasn't so sure.

Marcus started the next morning with the usual
zeal of a man suffering from a head injury; he lay
in bed for several hours after his alarm went off,
his head pounding too much to move even if moving
brought relief in the form of some pain meds. When
he finally did move, he felt like a broken toy,
moving shakily and making funny sounds. He didn't

think he could handle Hawthorne's only medical practice that day, and maybe not for another few years. He damn well needed a short reprieve, and comas didn't exactly count as vacation time in his book. His mind expectedly unable to clear itself of the throbbing headache on its own, he mumbled to himself as he finally rolled out of bed in search of relief.

"I wish someone would buy that damned building next door. It's been kept up pretty well for what it is. Sometimes I hate this fucking little speck of a town. A building like that would never sit empty in a real city."

Considering what he had just been through the day before, Nikki was a little surprised but definitely not shocked by the topic that first spilled out of Marcus's mouth.

"Why can't you just forget about the place and let the real estate brokers handle it?" She said, exhausted but now unable to sleep due to Marcus's well rehearsed mumblings filling her ears for the eight hundredth time in the past several years. She finally gave up on the hope of sleep and dropped her feet to the floor.

Still mumbling, he carried on. "Because those wonderful 'brokers' have been trying to unload the place for eight years now, and we could use that money to pay down my student loans. You know that as well as I do."

Nikki knew he had the right to complain because she had the same thing swirling through her mind most of the time these days. When they had gotten married four years earlier, they had assumed that the old Lemonte funeral home would sell eventually and help them make it financially through their first years. Or, at least make it until he had a practice set up and running smoothly. It all seemed like a big naive pipe dream now. Luckily the house had been in the inheritance along with the funeral home so they at least had a decent place to stay. But the daily struggle to keep the two pieces of property up and survive while they tried to get an income trickling into their account had put a tremendous strain on their quickly ailing marriage.

"How about some breakfast before you head off to the clinic?" she asked as she pulled on her robe, walked toward the door, and mentally tried to push their ever-looming financial problems out of her mind.

"Sounds O.K. If I can clear this headache, I'll be down in a minute."

As her feet hit the uncarpeted oak of the hallway floor, Nikki's thoughts miserably persisted to dwell on the funeral home next door. They needed to unload the damn thing and alleviate some of the stress from their lives. It didn't seem likely though, or at least, not to her.

Noon rolled around quickly for Marcus as the details of running the overwhelmingly busy Hawthorne Clinic battled with his headache for possession of his thoughts. His life always slipped from his control as soon as he walked into the place, and that alone made his stomach churn on a good day. Today was worse with the mess generated by the earthquake. Their house had been untouched by some freak of nature, but the clinic was a different story, charts having fallen to a jumble on the floor. The chaos of reorganization only added to his problems. Like most wannabe doctors, when he had gone to medical school, he had no concept of what a physician's life really entailed. It somehow still hadn't managed to sink in as he crawled through those four years of life, and he chose his specialty without any regard for the magnitude of the decision he had just made, greatly on the advice of people who also had no concept of what it was like to be a doctor. Three years of residency in family medicine brought the harsh reality partly home, as the responsibility of caring for people from cradle to grave quickly took over his life. Had he paid more attention to the workings around him, he would have realized in time to correct his mistake that the days of the much-revered family doc had been hopelessly lost for decades. It was too late now! With several years lost, a massive debt to his name and a wife he was now trapped by his early naiveté. Well... those few trivial things and the contract he had already

17

scrawled his nearly illegible signature onto months before he returned to Hawthorne about four years ago. The life absorbing practice would slowly be his as he gradually financed the lucrative retirement of old Doc Liston. To think he had once admired the guy, he should have gotten a good attorney before he made that crazy deal. But even that wouldn't have prepared them for the long stretch of time he was forced to pay a locums to keep up his practice or for his own phenomenal medical expenses incurred after the wreck. He had only recently been able to hobble back to work, and the place and the people were already beyond overwhelming. In fact, it seemed exponentially more chaotic now than before his accident, and it probably was after it had basically been running on autopilot during the long stretch he was out.

With a sudden lurch, he remembered the plans he had made for lunch with Nikki. Twelve-thirty already! He would be more than a half an hour late. Not a good note to start lunch on these days. But his headache, the earthquake, and the many other distractions cluttering up his mind were to blame. Who could handle all of this crap?

When he finally made it to Weatherby's, the little bar and greasy spoon that had become their occasional lunch spot over the past few years, he found she had already placed orders for them and was talking to the waitress about keeping their food warm until he showed up.

As a couple, Marcus and Nikki were superficially a perfect match. In fact, it had not always been just superficial. Both had blond-brown hair and complexions that easily darkened with the sun. Neither one disturbed the balance. When together, they merely complimented each other, and their physical appearances actually seemed to radiate with the love that they had once intensely shared. The life of a doctor had never been an easy one, however, and Marcus's was far from an exception to this. Their marital problems were so severe now that their significant financial problems only seemed to be the tip of the iceberg. When they had first fallen for each other, neither had been remotely prepared for the greedy monster

medicine would become in their lives. Marcus
gradually drifted into the hospital life, and Nikki
eventually had to fill her time in other ways.
Having been abandoned as a child, she had a
constant need for companionship in her life, and
this only added to probably the biggest problem of
all in their marriage. Marcus had an almost
depthless vein of jealousy which, although
extremely unreasonable considering his obligations,
never the less reared its ugly head regularly.
Sure, he could control his feelings under most
conditions. But Nikki seemed to have a peculiar
way of pushing the issue that often and easily sent
him into flying fits of rage. She just didn't
understand that she shouldn't wave the flag of
potential infidelity in front of his face so
frequently and so fiercely, insecure or not. Being
away at work all day and almost constantly on call,
he developed a belief that he had a good reason to
mistrust her. The paranoia that had been evolving
since his accident didn't help by any means. This
day was just another brutal test of his tolerance
as Matthew Erickson casually approached their table
and took a seat beside Nikki.

"I took the liberty of inviting Matthew over
to our table to have lunch with us." Nikki said as
a glare issued from Marcus's face. "I really hope
you don't mind, Marcus. It was getting late and I
didn't think you were going to make it here."

"No, no, that's all right. A little
unexpected, but fine all the same." Marcus forced
out, agitatedly. He should have expected as much
from her, but it always struck him with the same
raw force. It was a good thing for her he didn't
have a bad temper.

Matthew, unable or unwilling to see the hatred
and disgust in Marcus's expression, eagerly dove
into a conversation with Nikki, centering on the
old funeral home of all things. The whole ordeal
made Marcus angrier by the second. On top of that,
they failed to involve him in their exclusive
little discussion, pushing his anger to the limit.
It wasn't that Matt was exceptionally devious, or
even that Marcus really hated him that much. In
fact, they had been best friends growing up here in

19

Hawthorne, and had even been college roommates for a while at Shawnee University. The true anger was toward Nikki. Marcus just couldn't believe that she was acting with such disregard for his feelings. He had to get away from them before he blew up in front of a whole restaurant full of his patients.

"Well, Nik..Matt, I've got to go. I'll talk to you later." he half sneered as he pushed away from the table.

"Don't leave yet, Marcus," Nikki said with only a faint touch of guilt. "You haven't even gotten to eat."

"I'm not hungry now, Nikki. I'll see you later."

As Marcus stalked from the table without even kissing her, a small feeling of triumph welled up inside of him. He had gotten to her this time, he was sure of it. She deserved that and a lot more for bringing an intruder in on the small amount of time that they could share together. They would have to talk about it tonight. That is, if he didn't go out and have a few drinks before he went home.

Generally, Matt Erickson considered himself to be a normal, good-hearted person with no desire to hurt anyone. Having graduated from Shawnee University along with both Nikki and Marcus, his major concern in life was to succeed at the job he had, and to enjoy doing it of course. Going to college had been more of a way to escape from home for a while than anything else, since he had his father's clothing store to run when he got out. He had actually gotten a good education even though he didn't need it to do the job his whole life had been geared toward. Sure, the store turned a considerable profit every year, but it did this without the need of his education and definitely without a challenge intellectually. He knew he would soon grow tired of the store and have to move on to something more rewarding just to be able to function.

When Matt had gone to college, his main priority had actually been to find a wife before he graduated and returned to his little hometown. In

this, he had been set back a ways when he found
Nikki. A small problem had kept him from ever
having her: Marcus... Marcus had found her first
at a party or in one of his many tours of the bars,
and they had actually managed to stay together
since then. And now not only did Marcus still have
her, but she actually also loved him. Matt's life
had always been that way, what he wanted, he
couldn't have.

With Marcus and Nikki's move to Hawthorne,
Nikki seemed to have a continued interest in him,
and confusion had quickly taken over. It was
extremely unlikely that she would settle for a
common businessman now when she already had a
doctor who was undoubtedly on his way up in the
world. Just what the hell was she doing? He
hadn't been able to come up with a reasonable
answer, and yet, what was he to supposed to do? He
had always really liked her, even to the point of
love maybe, if he even knew what the hell love was.
Insidiously working his way into Marcus and Nikki's
marriage wouldn't be the ethical thing to do, but
Matt didn't really care about ethics. His life was
filled with loneliness, and he couldn't handle
another miserable minute of it. Besides, it would
be the challenge he needed to offset his boring
career. If he mastered the challenge, he would get
the woman he had been interested in for the past
ten years. If not, he wouldn't lose a thing. A
fun challenge at the worst, and with it his life
had become a little more interesting. With this
firmly in mind, he indulged wholeheartedly in his
conversation with Nikki as Marcus left the
restaurant and headed for who knew where. Who knew
and who really gave a shit anyway, Matt thought.

Later in the day, as Marcus's rage was slowly
quashed with each gulp of beer, he tried to think
about anything other than Nikki and Matt. They
were up to something behind his back and he
couldn't quite keep focused on figuring it out now.
Back in his undergrad days, drinking three pitchers
of beer hadn't been a problem, but he was finding
that his limit fell way below that now. He had

already achieved the old queasy feeling in his stomach and a massive buzz to go along with it and he was only halfway through his second pitcher. The barkeep hadn't given him a second look with the tips he had been sending his way, even though he knew for a fact that his patron was the town doctor. Times were a little tough in this town, and Hawthorne was far better off than most of the Shawnee Nation. A few extra bucks here and there were clearly the price of discretion. Unfortunately, the sleepless nights of residency had turned him into a real wimp, hungrier for sleep than a good time. What had the world come to when he couldn't even drink his favorite beverage to his hearts content? Oh well...as long as he drowned his sorrows and pacified the near constant anxiety that had crept into his life since the wreck. Besides, it still tasted better than xanax.

When he finally finished off his second pitcher, Marcus had hit the point where he could have easily fallen asleep in the bar and woken up twelve hours later still drunk and spinning like a top. Stumbling out the door, his stomach sent him an impulse to throw up and make it all better. As the beer swirled back into his throat from the far reaches of his stomach, some greater drive forced him to choke it back down keeping warm regurgitated beer off his shoes. Miserably, he began the painstaking search for his car. He knew it had to be out here somewhere. How else could he have gotten to the damn bar? What kind of car did he have anyway...he couldn't even remember now....

Gradually, the picture of an old, beige Cherokee Si-qua appeared in his head, and the need to look for it quickly followed. Where had he left the old pig? Maybe it was off wallowing in some mud.

"Here piggy piggy." He yelled out.

He smiled to himself. He should have been a comedian. Then making his way from car to car, occasionally tripping over a hidden wire some demon had planted to discourage his search, Marcus eventually came to the conclusion that his Si-qua had been stolen.

"Hwhy me...hwhy do they always pick on mee..."

were the only words he was capable of getting out now as he struggled desperately to think of the way home. His house was actually only eight blocks from the bar, but the moon seemed a hell of a lot closer right now. Slowly making his way in what he thought was the right direction, Marcus quickly forgot about his pig. "True signs of a drunk" would have been his opinion had it been anyone else. Even if he might be a mostly dry alcoholic, he was extremely functional, and had accomplished more already in his life than the general population would get done in several lifetimes.

Catching hold of a rare bit of luck, he was traveling in the right general direction for home. He could make it if he had to, he didn't need the pig. He used to walk this little stretch without a problem when he was a kid. Getting away from both his house and the funeral home had always been the best reasons he knew to head to Main Street. But now, plodding drunkenly towards the outskirts of town, the sidewalk kept meeting his feet quicker than it registered in his wasted brain. With a sudden lurch, his body hit the ground with an impact that would have shattered a nursing home full of elderly hips. Fortunately, he had a few years before he fell into that category, and as drunk as he was, he didn't even have time to try to catch himself. The blood gushing from his busted lip didn't taste too good though. As he stumbled to his feet, he wished he had another beer to wash it down.

As he neared his house, the thought of having to pass the old funeral home slapped a little drunken fear into him that he was in no condition to ignore. Sure, in his younger days, the days of his father and grandfather, he had practically lived in the old place. The fear still held him though, just as it had gripped him mindlessly in his childhood. There seemed to be no escape from the place. But then, how could he escape from the shadow of death and its never-ending presence.

Glancing up at the funeral home, a chill raced down Marcus's spine sending him into a wild panicked frenzy. The dark windows filled his mind with images that hadn't been dredged up since his

last days in the creepy old place. He had seen so
many dead people in there! It was the house of the
dead and a flood of thoughts pushed him over the
edge. Had the crumbling blind in one of the top
floor windows moved? It had to be a trick of the
light and his intoxicated brain! It didn't matter,
it still sent him into a hard sprint for his house,
his gut churning in punishment for the beer he had
fed it. Past the funeral home, the fear continued
to well up and drive his weary legs faster. But
the closer his growing house became, the more his
imagination took over. Suddenly, he heard a plague
of footsteps behind him and closing quickly.
Terrified and gasping for breath, he finally hit
his front yard and then his porch seconds later.
Clawing at the doorknob, a sudden jab to his mind
was acknowledgement that the door was locked and
the pounding footsteps behind him were rapidly
surrounding him. The footsteps began to pound in
his ears, and he only realized that he was steadily
beating on his own hardwood door with his bare
fists when the pain eventually hit him.

Nikki's startled face appeared unexpectedly
through the curtain, and his fear welled up further
as a tear slid down his cheek. Nikki pulled the
door open and was hit by the full force of his body
knocking her to the ground as he dove into the
house slamming the door wildly behind him.

"What's wrong, honey..." Nikki gasped as she
found herself sprawled out on the floor.

"window….home…..moved…..footsteps.." spewed
from Marcus's mouth in short gasping spurts as he
lay breathlessly next to Nikki on the floor of the
foyer.

Suddenly registering the overwhelming cloud of
alcohol that flooded the room with his gasps, Nikki
angrily said, "You're drunk, Marcus! Where the
hell have you been? I've been worried sick!
What's wrong with you anyway? You look like you've
seen a ghost!"

As his breathing finally slowed, Marcus felt a
sudden gut wrenching impulse to throw up.
Scrambling for the bathroom, a sink, or anything
besides the front door, the impulse turned to
reality. Beer gushed from his stomach to his

throat to the floor and splattered onto everything within twenty feet. Still running for the sink, Marcus continued his wild retching spree for several more minutes before Nikki recovered from her own nauseated disgust and went to him.

Her anger starting to shift to worry, Nikki asked, "Are you going to be all right, Marcus? You're really scaring me! I know you've been drinking, but this is way out of hand!"

"Just leave me alone, Nikki," Marcus blurted out still feeling sick, but now a wretchedly miserable and wide-awake drunk, "I don't want to talk about it tonight."

"O.K., Marcus, if that's the way you want it... I'm going to bed. I hope you don't plan on sleeping with me tonight!"

Continuing to vomit up the last remnants of beer from his otherwise empty stomach, Marcus managed to whisper out "Go to bed, Nikki....I'm staying in here tonight."

Leaving the bathroom in a flare of rage, Nikki wondered what the hell was wrong with him all of a sudden. Even taking into account the fall and the hit to his head he had taken the day before, she had noticed his behavior had been a little strange at noon. But why in the hell was he acting like this now, wasted out of his head, and still responsible for his patients. They were massively in debt and he couldn't afford to lose his license to practice. Maybe he had been slammed by an exceptionally hard day at work. Yes...that had to be it. Nothing else seemed reasonable. She hadn't done anything to warrant this. She couldn't do anything about it tonight anyway. She could worry about it in the morning. There was just nothing she could do for him when he was so wasted. She was exhausted anyway after her previous sleepless night, and the fatigue only dulled her ability to think. Tomorrow would be a new day, and their problems weren't going anywhere tonight, except maybe in gushing spurts down the toilet.

After suffering through the misery of dry heaves for several hours, Marcus eventually crawled to the couch in the living room. Nikki had probably been asleep now for hours, but his chances of making it to their bed over what would feel like a hundred miles up the stairs dismally slipped away as his stomach continued to grind. When he finally thought he could close his eyes, bed spins brought him bolt upright before he could think of falling asleep. Racing back to the bathroom, he heaved uselessly several more times before collapsing to the floor. His stomach briefly calmed, he passed out and the blackout obliterated the pain.

Ten hours later, Marcus came to on the bathroom floor with a taste worse than burnt excrement in his mouth.

"This is going to be one hell of a shitty day." He muttered to himself as he scraped himself up from the space surrounding the toilet. 'I'll never ever drink again' spun from his thoughts. But of course he would. He always did, and deep down inside his brain, he knew it. He had already used that line more than a thousand times, and this wouldn't be the last time. Disgusted with himself, he thought how did it go, something to the tune of eighty percent of all college students picked up social drinking or worse by the time they graduated. And he knew that once it was picked up, it remained for life.

Stumbling out of the downstairs bathroom in the clothes he had worn to work the day before, Marcus managed to mumble, "Where's the damn Pepto Bismol? I know we have some around here somewhere. It had better still be here!" he finally mumbled, painfully remembering that Nikki couldn't stand the dull pink syrup.

Still mumbling to himself, he stumbled back into the bathroom to look for his pink salvation. "How about wives... They had a way of entering your life and destroying everything you'd held sacred since the beginning. Just like his old golf shoes. When she bought him the new ones, she threw out the perfectly good old ones he had worn for over nine years. He could have killed her. Where did she get off anyway, making drastic decisions without even asking him how he felt about it?"

A few slammed cabinet doors later, he finally

gave up on the Pepto Bismol, and headed for the kitchen and his old substitute. Cold milk would do it. It had usually calmed his stomach before, and there was no reason this time would be any different. After pouring the milk, he franticly gulped it down. Seconds later, a horrendously violent heave came from the depths of his tortured stomach as the milk was not accepted for delivery. But since he wasn't drunk this time, he made it to the sink and managed to liquidly violate a sink full of recently washed dishes.

"Crap! I can't believe this! I really have wimped out." Gurgled from his acidy, milk-covered mouth.

Somehow grabbing a trash bag, he stumbled toward the living room couch. Passing the hallway storage nook and seeing his stethoscope, he painfully thought of work. When Nikki made it down for breakfast, she could call the clinic again and tell them he'd be a few hours late. There was no way he could handle being around all of Hawthorne's desperately needy sick people right now. The clinic was a nightmare at best when he was healthy.

Quickly slipping back into a much needed but restless sleep, Marcus didn't hear Nikki as she came down the uncarpeted oak stairs. But seeing him all curled up on the couch with his trash bag tucked under his chin, Nikki's first impulse was to laugh. This was the first time she had seen him this sick since they were married. With the exception of the accident, Marcus was never sick, and the thought of a doctor being worse off than most of his patients on account of his own stupid behavior was actually pretty funny.

"Marcus... Marcus." she said as she gently shook him awake. "Aren't you going in to the clinic today?"

Barely managing to register her presence over his trash bag, Marcus groaned, "Call in for me, Nik. I'm not up to it right now."

Stepping quickly back from his wretched alcohol and puke infested breath, Nikki was overwhelmed with disgust and harped.

"Well, well, well. I'd say you're lucky that people don't expect you to be even marginally

functional after that wreck. Most people don't get
away with this kind of stupid and reckless
behavior, and you won't for much longer. What
would your patients think if they saw you like
this?"

"Just shut the hell up and leave me alone,
Nikki. I can't deal with your bullshit right now."

Smirking, and looking away, she said, "O.K.
You don't have to get so testy. You did this to
yourself, you know."

"Maybe." He whispered.

Immediately enraged, she said, "Don't tell me
you're blaming this one on me. I wasn't there
pouring beer down your throat was I? Was I!"

Ignoring her outburst, he whispered, "Just go
call in, Nik. My patients can wait, and we'll talk
about this later when I feel up to it."

It was just like him to blame his own idiotic
behavior on her, Nikki thought as she went
dutifully to the kitchen phone. He would regret
this later. She had no doubt because it was always
like this. He would eventually apologize even if
she had been in the wrong. It was weak and pitiful
on his part and she didn't know the reasoning
behind it, but she was sure it was deliberately
intended to make her feel guilty in some twisted
way. As much as she tried to stifle the guilty
feelings, they always surfaced, and it made her mad
as hell.

Forcefully composing herself for the call,
when the clinic picked up she managed to say,
"Hello, this is Nikki Lemonte. Dr. Lemonte won't
be in until later today."

"What's wrong, Mrs. Lemonte?" The chubby
little receptionist got out before Nikki could hang
up the phone.

Nosy people, can't they just listen to what
they're told and accept it without question, Nikki
thought as she reached into the refrigerator for a
couple of eggs. Their lives weren't on display for
everyone and their mother to scrutinize. What was
wrong with people these days? Maybe it was the
small town that brought it out. People sure hadn't
acted like this when she was in college. Of course
in school, she had gradually lost contact with all

of her friends as she spent more and more time with
Marcus. It had seemed like the right thing to do
at the time, even if she regretted it now. Even if
she had spent more time with her friends, they
wouldn't be here for her now. This rinky-dink
little shit town pretty much squashed her social
life. At least she still had Matt to talk to.
Matt had been a good and reliable friend since she
had known him. She could sense that he would like
a little more than friendship at times, but she
would never allow that to happen. Even though she
and Marcus had a lot of problems, she had grown to
love him more than anyone she had ever known. She
couldn't understand why he couldn't see it. How
could he be jealous of anyone else when he was the
one she had chosen to marry? Sometimes his thought
process was too distorted for her to figure out.
It didn't seem reasonable that a person of his
intelligence would be swallowed up by such horrible
jealousy. Besides, he couldn't expect her to give
up the only friend she had left. That was pure and
unadulterated selfishness on his part, and only
managed to make her mad.

Having scrambled her eggs, Nikki sat down to
eat them with toast and have a cup of coffee. But
a rustling sound and a muffled scream nearly blew
her out of her skin and made her knock her plate
off the table. Before she realized it, she was
running into the living room to check on Marcus.
His demeanor had changed and he now sat disheveled
and trembling at the end of the couch with a wild
look in his eyes, sweat pouring down his face, and
his trash bag clenched in both hands.

"Marcus, are you all right? What happened?"

Wobbling from side to side, and clearly so
sick he could barely sit up, Marcus managed to
gasp. "It was....horrible. I...I've never had a
nightmare like that. It seemed so real..."

Even though she still felt a little distant as
a result of the last few days of crap, she wrapped
her arms around his sweat-drenched body, and did
her best to comfort him.

"Tell me about it, Marcus. It'll make you
feel better." Nikki whispered, knowing full well
that it wasn't the truth. If nothing else, her few

psych classes in college had taught her that. Reliving trauma was generally in itself traumatic, and could be perceived as magnitudes worse than the original insult. Depending on a person's personality structure and coping skills, the impact of something as simple as a fender bender could evolve into the equivalent of the apocalypse in their mind. She had never had any experiences like that herself beyond being abandoned as a child, but the lecture was still stuck firmly in her mind.

When Marcus finally did calm down, he managed to recount his dream before it slipped into nothingness. Still somewhat wide-eyed, he grabbed both of her hands, and stammered on as if into empty space.

"I was in bed...It wasn't our bed upstairs, but one somewhere I've been before. You weren't there with me, I was alone and that in itself scared the hell out of me. The room was black, but I could see everything in it as if my eyes had adjusted from being in the dark for a long time. Suddenly, the tension in my body welled up immensely and I cowered on the bed trying to absorb the room. My attention fell on a huge grandfather clock in one corner of the room. It was significant to me for some reason, but I couldn't figure out why. As I stared at the clock, I began to sense another presence on the opposite side of the room. I fought the compulsion to turn for as long as I could, but an eternity passed and I still felt the presence. It was getting stronger and I started to smell something that made me nauseous. Unable to keep my eyes from it any longer, I turned abruptly toward the presence and started screaming. There was a dark figure in the corner. It was half-hidden in the shadows, but it was clearly there. Feeling an instinctive need to look away, I forced myself to look at another corner of the room, and screamed even harder! The figure was in both corners!

A twisted and malicious smile glared at me. Terrified, I turned to jump off of the bed, and really lost it. The figure was there blocking my way off of the bed!"

By this time, Marcus had wrapped himself

completely around Nikki, shaking and in tears.
Nikki could feel the disturbing harshness of his
fear. If she had dreamt this, she would have shit
her pants. He was simply vibrating with fear.

After several minutes of dreadful silence, she
managed to utter the only question that came to
mind.

"That place, do you know where it is?"

"I don't know, Nik......," he whispered, as
his mind struggled to grasp reality.

Several painfully silent minutes later, his
sudden outburst sent a burst of adrenaline through
Nikki's body.

"Wait! I knew the bed seemed familiar! When
I was a kid, I practically lived in the funeral
home in the summer. I had to sleep in a room on
the second floor. The bed's in the funeral
home....."

CHAPTER 3

On the side of Hawthorne that had become a
mobile home wasteland, Pete Blair walked out his
front door onto rotting steps. It was going to be
a great day, he thought. He could tell just by the
lack of stench in the air. Usually, he was greeted
by the foul smell of sewage from his own front
yard, but not today. That made any day a good one
in his eyes. If the wind was kind enough to blow
the nasty odors away from where he lived, there was
no telling what could happen that day. Pulling his
old bike out of the bush that functioned as his
kickstand, Pete took a short run and jumped onto it
like it was a running horse. A shaky moment later,
he was on his way to the newspaper office to pick
up his daily deliveries. It was payment day, and
that meant money in his pocket. The day was
usually a pain because people weren't home or
didn't leave the money like they were supposed to.
At the same time, it was the only money he ever
got, and it felt good to have a few bucks in his
pocket.

Running his route, the wind blowing on his

eleven-year-old face woke him up faster than anything. Wide-awake, his classes went a lot better every day. His grades were proof of that. Since he had been in school, his parents had pushed him to do the best he could. But his dad had died in a car wreck two years ago, and he only had his mom to push him on now. His father's death had been hard on him, and he hoped things never got any worse. Seeing his father in the coffin had made for a year of sleepless nights. He drifted through life like a zombie for even longer than that. He didn't remember when he finally got back to normal, but he knew one thing for sure. Dead people scared the bejesus out of him, and he didn't ever want to see a dead person up that close again.

Having made it through the morning, Marcus finally showered, dressed, and went out the back door to his car. If he'd any sense at all, he'd have just blown the whole day off. His head was still swimming in muck and his return to the clinic after the wreck had probably been extremely premature. But they had been bleeding money they didn't have, and the building stress had forced him back to work. Besides, he could do most of his work on autopilot at this point, even after the wreck. Checkups, earaches, and sore throats were the bread and butter of family medicine.

With a jolt, he stopped just short of the drive. Where was his damn car! It wasn't here! Nikki must have taken it when he was taking a shower. No problem, he thought. He hadn't driven her car for a while, and it would be a change. Not for the better, but a change. He had always hated driving her car. Old Cherokee Wi-sas just weren't his style and never would be. It drove worse than his old Si-qua did. He would have thought a cat would be more maneuverable than a pig, but that definitely wasn't the case. Even so, the Wi-sa still roared to life like it usually did, and Marcus started to back out of the drive. Glancing at the house, he saw Nikki move past the kitchen window. The alcohol had screwed up his brain, and he had obviously lost control of his senses. Nikki had taken his car, and couldn't be in the house.

Driving down the street, his thoughts returned to the past night. How in the hell had he gotten so drunk? He knew all of the physiology behind tolerance levels, but that wasn't enough to explain last night. Passing Vick's Bar and Grill, something clicked in Marcus's head. His ice blue BMW sat parked there in the street.

"Well, what do you know. I was even drunker than I thought I was last night." Considering how sick he had been, he knew this was a bit of an understatement.

Pulling to the side of the road, Marcus jumped out of the Wi-sa and ran into the bar to call Nikki. She wasn't going to believe this one.

"Hello, who is this? I must have the wrong number.." he said as he heard a male voice on the other end of the line.

"This is Matt, Matt Erickson, Marcus. I'm here to talk to Nikki about the dresses she wants me to look for." Matt answered nervously.

"Where is Nikki then? Why didn't she answer the phone?" Marcus shot back vehemently. He had barely left the damn house.

"Well......uh..I believe she's in the shower, Marcus." Matt answered even more nervously.

"How in the hell did you get in my house then?" Marcus screamed into the phone, stirring up a little attention in the bar, even at this early hour. "Or did she let you in and then decide to take a shower?"

"Now wait a minute, Marcus. I know what you're thinking, but nothing's going on here. I was outside knocking when I heard the phone ringing off the wall. The door opened when I pushed it, so I came in. Nikki doesn't even know I'm here." Matt eventually got out with a little force in is voice.

Grabbing control of himself before he yelled anymore, Marcus got out a simple "Tell her to call me at the office" before hanging up the phone.

"Ringing off the wall my ass, the phone only rang once!" He roared as he walked out the door. He knew the only thing that would calm him down now. The spare key in his wallet opened and started his BMW, and he screeched away from the

33

curb, barely missing a passing car. A good fast
drive would relieve his tension if he didn't manage
to get clipped by some asshole in an old beater.

The little sport sedan ripped onto the highway
without hesitation, and Marcus shredded through the
gears to reach top speed. Eating up the road was
his best stress relief mechanism, and probably the
only one that reliably did the job. A good run on
these twisty back roads was dangerous, but it sure
as hell took his mind off of his problems. The car
flew in and out of the curves and the sensations
made him wish he could do this for the rest of his
life. Before he realized it, the snake-like road
brought him back to the hill below Camel Rock.
With a shudder, he remembered the quake and the
near death experience that had scared the shit out
of him afterwards. His head still vibrated with
pain, and he couldn't tell if it was from his old
injury, his new injury, or his mildly lingering
hangover. Regardless of the cause, a surge of pain
nearly blinded him, and he whipped to the side of
the now gravel road barely avoiding a plunge into a
large weed-filled ditch. Damn the pain, he
screamed mentally as he struggled with the door
latch and finally broke free of his car. The pain
obliterated all reasonable thought, incessantly
peaking to a crescendo as he tripped over a small
rock at the top of the ditch and fell into a gaping
crevice newly formed by the recent quake. With a
mouth full of dirt and still blurred vision, he
found himself sprawled at the base of the wide rip
in the earth's surface.

"SHIT," he screamed, blowing part of the dirt
from his mouth and doubling the already unbearable
pain in his agonized brain. As the remaining dirt
turned to mud in his mouth, he tasted the
unmistakable ooze of blood, and vomited the vile
mixture impulsively before he had a chance to
swallow it. The stench of hotdogs and stale
popcorn took over his senses, and he knew what was
coming. He was going to have another seizure
within half a mile of the last one, and alone in a
fucking ditch. Life just wasn't fair…

Back in Hawthorne, the great day had gone sour

34

for Pete about half way through his morning route. Most of his deliveries hadn't been home to pay up. He hated going back in the evenings when it already ate up so much time in the first place. But if he wanted to get paid, he didn't have a choice.

Maybe, if he was lucky, he would see Dr. Lemonte. He had been really cool in the past. It made him want to do even better in school and be a doctor just like Dr. Lemonte. He always told him funny stories, and gave him a little advice when he needed it.

As Pete rode up to the Lemonte house, he saw that the garage was open, and both of their cars were gone.

"Darn! I guess it's too early for them to be home."

When he passed the funeral home, a sudden chill took over him as if someone had thrown a bucket of ice on top of him. He had never liked going by the old place, and he was glad that it was still light outside. He would be sure to go the long way around and miss the place when he came back to the Lemonte house. The rest of Pete's rounds went slowly for him since he couldn't wait to get back to the Lemontes. He hoped Dr. Lemonte would be there to answer the door, and not his wife. He didn't know why, but he just didn't like Mrs. Lemonte. There was something about her that didn't seem right. She could act nice to him, but it all seemed fake, like she didn't like him or kids in general. Well, at least Dr. Lemonte was nice to him, and he was the important one anyway.

Rousing himself from the ditch, Marcus looked around in confusion. What the hell was going on! What was he doing lying here covered in dirt! Slowly realizing the stiffness of his muscles and the bleeding bite marks on the sides of his tongue, his situation settled in with the weight of a few thousand bricks. Two seizures within three days was not good, not good at all… He had to think seriously about this now, and decide what he was going to do. The sleepy confusion tried to take him back under, but he fought it, and staggered out of the rough crevice. His limbs ached like he had been beaten repeatedly with a baseball bat, but he struggled up to the road, and his car before he had a chance to pass out. The tastes of blood and dirt filling his mouth, he tried his best to focus on these putrid reminders of what had just happened as he clumsily started the BMW. The twenty some miles back to town were going to be rough, and he would be surprised if he made it safely. He couldn't stay here though. He had to get back to the house. Why was he all the way out here again anyway? There had to be a reason. This thought, and the continued rotten tastes still swirling in his mouth kept him mostly conscious as he slowly crept his way home.

Sleep…at home he could sleep…

Nearly an hour of forced but negligible concentration later, he pulled into their drive. The Wi-sa was gone… Nikki must be out somewhere…

Finally making it back to the Lemonte house, Pete saw that the blue car was back and just hoped it was Dr. Lemonte. Knocking on the door, he heard footsteps quickly approaching and an angry voice that was coming along with them.

Marcus, still covered with dirt and with dried blood streaking from his mouth to his chin, opened the door and saw Peter standing there waiting for his paper money.

"Wow, what happened to you!" Pete sputtered out before his brain could control his mouth.

Still tasting the bloody dirt, Marcus glanced down at his filthy work clothes, and couldn't clear his head well enough to answer with anything more than "How much do I owe you, Peter?"

"It's….it's one-twenty-five like always, sir."

"Oh yeah, I remember now." Marcus said, seeing the bewildered look on the boy's face. Without asking him in Marcus reached into his pocket and pulled out three bucks.

"Here, keep the change." He said as he reached back for the door handle and began to close the door. Now wasn't a good time to be chatting with the paperboy. He had barely made it into the house a while ago when he met Nikki, and an argument had started immediately.

"Thank you, sir." Pete got out with a lot of disappointment in his voice that he wasn't quite old enough to control.

As the door shut behind him, Pete walked to his bike and headed for home. Marcus returned to the kitchen where Nikki sat crying. There was probably as much sadness in Pete as there was anger in Marcus, but at least he had managed to control his feelings in front of the boy. He would get over his disappointment soon enough, but Marcus's anger would hang with him for a while. Only Nikki would see the anger if he could help it.

"Who was that?" Nikki snapped at Marcus as he entered the kitchen.

"It was Peter, the paperboy, and I'm glad I answered the door, for his sake." Marcus snapped back sarcastically.

"How can you be nice to that scummy little kid? I don't see any point in it."

"He's a good kid, Nikki, and if you don't like him, it's your problem. You should give the kid a chance. Besides, the boy wants to be a doctor someday, and he likes my advice every once in awhile."

Staring through her tears at the dirty, disheveled man in front of her, Nikki's voice came out cold, and no longer reverberated with her crying.

"You just like the kid because he builds up your ego, Marcus, and you know it. He probably won't even want to be a doctor when the time comes. Why don't you just get off your high horse, and put your energy someplace useful!"

This was getting to be too much for Marcus. They were even arguing about the paperboy now. What was their marriage coming to? They had always argued about stupid things, but never this stupid.

"Just shut up about the kid, Nikki! This is about you and Erickson, and don't try to get off the subject!" Marcus screeched, boiling over more than he really wanted to.

"I'm not changing the subject because there's no subject to change. I've told you a thousand times that there's nothing between Matthew and me. Why can't you see that? I never have felt anything

37

for the man, and I can't see that I ever will, unless you keep pushing with this paranoid fantasy of yours."

The 'unless' threw Marcus over the edge, and without thinking twice, he stormed out the back door again to the garage. With massive bursts of adrenaline now feeding his rage, the postictal fatigue that had barely allowed him to make it home a little while ago was lost to the storm. Throwing a shower of rocks that probably took their share of paint, he backed out of his gravel drive, and his BMW was flying down the road again before he even realized he was in the car. Suddenly thinking clearly, even though the tension and anger were still digging at his mind, he whipped the car around and headed back for the house. He was way too angry to talk to Nikki, but he couldn't be racing through town like this. He had to calm down.

A sudden urge to go into the funeral home hit him as he pulled within sight of it, and he was too angry to see the stupidity of going through with it. He was out of his car and at the back loading doors before he realized what he was doing. A chill took hold of his body as he touched the cold door handle, and he realized that there was no way that he was going to go into that place right now. It was already almost dark outside, giving the place a sinister appearance that it halfway maintained throughout the sunniest day of the year. He hadn't been in there for over nine years, and he wasn't about to spawn a new series of nightmares like the one he had experienced that morning.

As Marcus abruptly turned to walk back to the car, he caught a glint of light shining from inside the building. That was impossible! None of the realtor's cars were here. They were the only ones with keys, and enough nerve to go into the place, all in the name of money of course. Someone was in there, and he had to break his nine-year streak and do something about it!

Turning back to the door, he ignored the chills in favor of the fear that had taken charge of him. The door unlocked easily, and he pushed it open as quietly as possible. If someone was here,

he didn't know what he would do. What if they had
a gun? They could attack and kill him before he
even caught sight of them.

The door made an unexpected squeal just as it
hit the sidewall. The huge room at the back of the
place was exactly as he remembered, and it still
scared the hell out of him. Leaving the door open
and trying to get through the room as fast as he
could, he cracked his elbow on one of the many
tables that filled the room. The pain shot up his
arm, and he broke into the hallway stifling a wince
of pain. Darkness surrounded him, and he kicked
himself for not stopping to look before he ran into
the hall. A few seconds of intense concentration
brought the gravity of his situation back to him.
He would have to check the front rooms where the
glint of light had come from. Cautiously passing a
few other rooms, he prayed that he wouldn't find
anything. The pounding of his own heart muffled
the sound of his footsteps in his head. Nothing
yet, but the tension was building, and not just in
him. The whole place seemed to reverberate with
dread. As his eyes slowly became accustomed to the
darkness, every shadow took on a life of its own.
A movement in the room to his right caught his
attention. He heard a sound. A footstep...it had
been a footstep! Turning back, fear became panic,
and he had to get the hell out of there. Another
footstep echoed in his mind as he heard the muffled
slam of the closing back door. The weight of the
building fell on his head and blackness filled his
eyes. He heard a wicked echo of laughter as he
lost consciousness, the dreaded smell of hotdogs
and popcorn leading his way.

Nikki cried even harder as Marcus stormed out
their back door. He was right. What was their
marriage coming to? They were fighting almost
every day now, and the fights were getting more and
more serious. He had been kind of different since
pulling out of the coma, but that wasn't a good
excuse. He was mostly the same, and his knowledge
of medicine and ability to work hadn't been
affected. Something had to be done about it, but
what? She didn't seem capable of working it out by

39

herself. He was going to have to put some effort in, too.

But then, knowing exactly what he was going to do when he left made Nikki very uneasy. Every time he got mad about something, he took off in his car and did the stupidest thing he was probably capable of. Right now, he was hitting the highway and whipping down the road as fast as his little blue sports car would let him. It was without a doubt the stupidest thing he had ever heard of him doing in his life, and he was taking off on his dangerous road runs more than ever now.

Even though they were fighting all of the time now, she still loved him. These arguments were definitely going to have to stop. Then, maybe she would be able to trust his driving again, if nothing else.

When Marcus's car roared to life and the sound of its racing engine disappeared down the street, Nikki had a horrible gut feeling that something bad was going to happen to him this time. She had never noticed it before, and it scared the hell out of her to think that she was feeling it now.

Nikki suddenly felt a desperate need to talk to someone. Pulling herself from her chair, she walked across the kitchen to the phone.

Hedda Krepp could help ease her concerns, and maybe even give her some insight into the situation. She had been a good friend since they had moved into town, and her advice was usually helpful.

"Hello, is this Hedda?" she said into the phone, returning to tears as she said it.

"Yes, how are you doing, Nikki? Is there something wrong?" Hedda asked in her kindly voice.

"I'm afraid I've got a problem, Hedda, and I really need to talk to somebody. Do you think you could get away from the store and come over here for awhile?" Nikki asked, the tears flowing freely again.

"Well..yes...yes, I guess I could. Just give me a few minutes to talk to Ray and then I'll be over, O.K."

"Thank you, Hedda, I'll be waiting. Bye."

Seven minutes later, Hedda was knocking at the

Lemonte's front door and a little out of breath. Still wearing the apron she usually wore at the corner store, there was a worried look on her face that Nikki immediately saw as she opened the door.

"Nothing's that bad, Hedda," Nikki said as she smiled through her tears and Hedda quickly came through the door, "Marcus and I have just had another in our growing series of arguments, and I could really use someone to talk to and maybe give me some advice."

Still smiling and the tears now slowing to a stop, Nikki gave Hedda a short hug and felt the need to immediately open her life up before Hedda had a chance to change her mind and leave.

"We've been arguing almost constantly and Marcus is so closed off to me now. How can I get what's really bothering him out in the open?"

"Well, Nikki, if you've really been arguing that much, it could very well be something serious. It would help if you could tell me as much as you feel comfortable with. I don't know if I'll be able to help, but I'll sure do what I can."

Having lived with a psychiatrist for more years than she could count now, Hedda's layman's grasp on psychology was pretty solid. Ray would have been able to do a better job giving her advice, but his health had taken him out of the game already, and she wasn't about reopen the door and tempt him back.

Walking into the living room, Nikki asked Hedda if she would like anything to drink before they started their talk. With Hedda politely refusing, they sat down beside each other on the couch and Nikki started into the story of the Lemonte relationship.

"To begin with, we were both still in school; he in his second year of medical school, and me in my second year as a business major. The timing, in that respect, was pretty good really, because we were both out of school at about the same time, even though he had three years of residency to do after that."

"Yes, I met Ray under similar circumstances." Hedda interrupted.

Comforted a little by this, Nikki went on.

"We met initially through a mutual friend of ours at a party one night in the fall. I honestly didn't think much of Marcus at the time because I had another boyfriend then and wasn't really looking for anyone. I'm not sure what he thought of me on that first meeting, and we didn't even talk then. It was just a quick introduction and that could have easily been the end of it forever."

Hedda smiled, it clearly hadn't ended there.

"About a week later, the same friend invited all of us to another party, which turned out to be a really strange one thrown by a bunch of freaks who had collected in the Shawnee Forest over the years. Anyway, there still wasn't any magic or even anything close to it between us. I know that may sound strange to you because it seems strange to me now. We still didn't talk, and I thought that he was probably too quiet for me anyway. The night ended just as weird as the party, and he kind of disappeared, I guess. I'm not really sure what happened to him, but I don't think I really cared then either.

We happened to be at a few more parties, and I gradually got to know at least who he was. After another few months, my boyfriend and another jerk that I dated for a short time were completely down the drain, and Marcus somehow found out and asked me out on a date. After having just been burned by a couple of guys, I was afraid to get serious with him at first, but I guess that changed in time. I gradually found out how much he cared for me, and unexpectedly realized with the aid of a few of our mutual friends that he had no intentions of hurting me. Of course, I found out on my own over the course of four or five months, but they had all been right. Putting my guard down, I slowly fell in love with him, and grew to love him more and more every day. He felt the same way, but he also seemed to be on a faster schedule than I was. The more he loved me, the more I fell in love with him, and he pulled me a little deeper every day.

After our slow start, we made it through the next year O.K., or at least without too many hard times. If I think back on it now though, what I considered hard times back then were nothing compared to the problems that we have now. It's funny how your perspective changes in just the short period of a few years. Anyway, it was about that time that Marcus introduced me to his old friend from home, Matt Erickson. Home was here in Hawthorne for both of them, which I find good now that Matt is such a good friend. They had met back up in the hospital while Matt's father slowly died of cancer.

I don't really know why we became such a good friends. Looking back on it though, I guess it was due to me thinking it would make Marcus happy if I got along with his friends. Then, of course there's the fact that he was really the first outside contact I had gotten with the world since I had started dating Marcus. He was also pretty depressed about his father, and having been an orphan myself, I could easily sympathize with his loss.

As time went on, and Marcus's residency took up a lot of his time, I started to spend more of my time with Matt. I didn't see why Marcus would care with them having been friends for so long. Of course, Marcus was always a possessive and jealous man, and I suppose he still is. He has just learned to hide it better now than what he did back in those days. He didn't ever say anything about it, but then, he wasn't around to say much of anything. When he wasn't working, he was out on his long drives, which I didn't and still don't understand."

Pausing for a second to blow her nose, Nikki asked, "Do you want anything to eat or drink yet, Hedda? I know I've probably about worn your ears out already, and I need something to drink before I can continue with this."

"Well, yes. I guess I could use a cup of coffee now. I guess I didn't realize that you were going to start so far back and this was going to be such a long talk." Continuing with a huge smile, Hedda tried to smooth over what she had just said. "Don't get me wrong, dear. I want to hear everything that you'll tell me. From there, I'll see if I can be of any help to you. You know, sometimes it really does just take another person's

43

view of something to figure out what the problem is."

Not having noticed, Nikki stood up and started to whisk out of the room, saying as she went, "Just a second, Hedda, and I'll have your coffee. Do you drink anything with it, or do you take it black?"

"I usually take it black, Nikki. That will cause you the least trouble and suit me just fine."

A few minutes later, Nikki returned to the living room with two cups of coffee and a few cookies. Sitting down, she began the rest of her story without hesitation.

"Where was I now? Oh yes, I remember. Eventually, Matt's father died and it basically felt to me like he had moved away. All I had then was Marcus, and things got a little better because he started to spend more time with me instead of his car. Those drives have always made me mad. I worry too much sometimes, and his drives are probably the main cause of it. He never drives recklessly or does anything stupid when I'm riding with him, but I can imagine what he's like on his own, and it really scares me.

Then a little over four years ago, his mother died unexpectedly. His father had died when he was still in high school. I think it was a heart attack or something like that. Anyway, his mother had been all that he had left, and when she died, it hit him pretty hard. She was only fifty-eight years old, and her death was as much of a shock to Marcus as his father's death had been.

She had been trying to get rid of the funeral home next door ever since her husband's death and that was where she died. She was reportedly helping to show a prospective buyer around the place when she somehow slipped and fell down a flight of stairs. The guy rushed her to the nearest hospital, but there was nothing they could do for her. She died of a massive brain hemorrhage shortly after arriving at the emergency room."

Hedda grimaced. She had gone to school with both of Marcus's parents before she moved away to Chicago with her parents. Her mental images of them were still as little kids, and imagining them dying was a harsh thought.

44

"I hope you don't think I'm stupid or anything, but ever since her death, I haven't stepped foot in that old place. There's something about the place that definitely feels wrong. I didn't tell you this before, but that's where they found Marcus's dad years ago. Marcus found him keeled over and already dead one evening after school in one of the back rooms. Both of his parents have died in that creepy old place, and we can't stand the fact that we still own it. Marcus won't go near there anymore either. I don't think he's even been in there since he found his father dead, to tell you the truth, and I think he's afraid that he'll die there somehow too if he goes back. Even though it's probably ridiculous, I've grown to be just as frightened of it."

Still picturing Marcus's parents as dead little children, Hedda had no difficulty understanding Nikki's fear.

"It took him some time to get over his mother's death, and right after that, he abruptly proposed to me. I think he wanted to try to gain back some of the security that he had lost with her death. It didn't matter to me though by then, because I loved him so much that I would have married him under much worse circumstances.

Since we had already been together for almost 5 years, we had a really short engagement. It seemed we had been going out long enough that there wasn't any need to hold off on the marriage. And then the wedding was really strange. Except for a few friends, there was hardly anyone there from either of our sides. Not that it mattered to me, I was used to being without family, but I could tell that it was kind of hard on him. The whole wedding was strained and uncomfortable, to say the least.

Afterwards, we didn't have the time or the money to go on a honeymoon with him coming to the end of his residency. We still haven't gotten away on a honeymoon or even taken a vacation for that matter. It's not a big deal, but it does add to the growing oddity of our marriage.

When he signed the contract and we came to Hawthorne, we hoped things would settle out for us. They did start to get better after awhile as the practice we were slowly buying stabilized and even grew a little. Just as we were finally planning to get away for awhile and Marcus was cross-covering for his friend so we would have backup coverage while we were gone, Marcus was nearly killed in that horrible pileup. They said he did briefly die, but they managed to bring him back. That happened before I even knew there was an accident. By the time Matt drove me over to the hospital, they had Marcus in surgery and didn't know if he would pull through. If he did, he was still in a coma with a head injury they warned me and they couldn't predict how functional he would be if he came out of it. I didn't have much hope. The ICU staff stayed away from me as much as they could and if it hadn't been for Matt, I don't know if I could have dealt with any of it. That was all two years ago and not long I guess before you moved into town and opened the corner store back up."

"Yes, I vaguely remember hearing about it then. But we were so busy and I guess I never realized how bad things were." Hedda said apologetically, but was actually thinking back on that time with happiness.

"Matt continued to keep me going as Marcus came out of the coma and miraculously recovered over the next year and a half. I had been advised by one of his doctors to get a locums for the clinic and to keep it running. I did that and Marcus's own medical bill began to quickly pile up. The time crept by and Marcus eventually came home. It was still another half a year before he was able to start working again. Very few people involved with his care ever believed he would make it back that far. The most significant changes really just seemed to be his occasional staring spells, some strange and uncharacteristic irritability, and most obviously, an intense hatred of Matt that was nearly the opposite of his prior feelings. I don't know what he imagined went on between us while he was away and sick, but I tried to assure him nothing had. He went back to his long drives not long ago and now he's taken off on one of them again. And worse than that, today I have this strange feeling something is going to happen to

46

him. I'm worried sick, but to tell you the truth, if we don't stop fighting soon, I don't think our marriage will make it through the year. Lately, we've been arguing over the stupidest things. Today it was the paperboy. Yesterday it was something else just as stupid. It doesn't look like there will ever be an end to it. I really hate to argue with him, and this is all driving me crazy. I don't think that he wants to be arguing either because he went out a couple of nights ago and came back so drunk that he even had what seemed to be a waking nightmare on the way home. " Nikki stopped and again blew her nose.

Sitting quietly for several minutes, Hedda finally said, "I don't really know what to tell you, Nikki. An argument every now and then has to be expected. You will have to stop your arguments if you think they're hurting your marriage, of course."

"Yes, I realize that, but these past few months have pushed it to an extreme for both of us, and I think we both realize it.

I just can't see what I'm doing so wrong that is making him mad all of the time, and he doesn't really do anything out of his way to make me mad as far as I can tell, but I don't know. He does tell me not to do some things that I just can't seem to keep from doing. It's not that I do them to defy him, they're just things that I feel I have to do, and I won't let him tell me not to. Maybe that's being childish on my part, but I don't think that I care if I act like a baby sometimes."

"Maybe you should try to listen to what he says for awhile and see if the arguments stop. If they do, you'll know what the problem is, and you'll be able to make some kind of a compromise. If not, something major might be wrong with your relationship that needs professional counseling which I, being no expert, can't help you with. Try it though, and see what happens. At least when you're arguing you're talking and he's not off in his car somewhere."

This now brought a grimace to Nikki's face, and she quickly said, "There's one other thing that I forgot to tell you, Hedda. Marcus had this terrible dream the other night, and it turned out to have something to do with the funeral home. I'm afraid that something bad is going to happen soon, and I don't want to even think about what it might be. That place is a definite dark spot in his life, and we don't seem to be able to get rid of it. If we don't sell it soon, I think that I would rather sell this house and move away from here so that we don't have to look at it everyday."

Standing up and handing Nikki her empty coffee cup, Hedda gave her a brief hug and said, I heard stories as a kid, of course, but I didn't realize that the old place had such a recent past. Even so, I'm not really the superstitious type, and I don't think that you should be worrying too much about it. I'm sure that if you worry about anything too much, your mind can conjure up all kinds of wild ideas."

"I suppose that you're right. But I still get the chills with the mere thought of that place, and worse than that, I sometimes really resent his decision to move us back here. We could have found a house anywhere, and inheriting these places hasn't really helped us out financially."

"Well I for one am glad that you're here, dear. I'll help any way I can, even if it's just to listen."

As they walked to the door, Nikki thanked her for coming over and she was soon alone again with her thoughts, crying and unsure what she should do next.

A sneeze caused by the thick layer of dust pulled Marcus out of his stupor as he woke to find himself on the floor of the funeral home's back hall. A prevailing sense of doom gnawed at his brain, and he was more confused than he had ever been before. Looking around timidly, he tried to pull himself to his knees. The first real thought that came to his mind was 'what the hell happened', and then he was on the floor again. He was weak and sore beyond belief for some reason. How long had he been out.....hours?

With some effort, Marcus lifted his arm to look at his watch. There wasn't enough light to see the time. Another try at standing up brought him groggily to his feet. He had to get out of here. It was starting to close in on him and he couldn't take any more than what had already happened, whatever it was....

Making it to the back room and his escape to the outside world, his nerves took over and he painfully began to run. A second later, he was out the door with his footsteps still echoing mockingly behind him.

Not even stopping to look back at the place, he dove into his car and fumbled for his keys. His pockets were empty... He had lost them... They had to be on the floor in the funeral home!

Leaning on the steering wheel in exhausted defeat, the almost inaudible clink of metal came to his ears. The keys were in the ignition where he had left them. Relief poured through his body as the engine roared to life and his car raced to escape from behind the funeral home.

Never again would he go into that place. Not even if it meant his or Nikki's life.

CHAPTER 4

"But I don't want a subscription to your damn magazine!" Matt impatiently blurted out as he slammed the phone to its cradle. He hadn't been having the best day, and pushy salesmen weren't what he wanted to deal with right now. What he needed was a hot shower and a good meal. The only problem was, he hadn't had the time to put a shower in his house yet, and he would either have to cook for himself, or drive twenty miles to get respectable food and treatment. Why did he come back to this little hick town anyway?

All right, so there was the store. Big deal! The store was little more than a massive rummage sale, with outdated and second quality clothes stacked from floor to ceiling. It was like a rat's maze, and it was so hard to get around all the customers sometimes that he thought some traffic lights and overpasses might help. The customers

flocked in from all of the surrounding river
Nations like they would have to run around naked if
they didn't. But the majority were from his own
Shawnee Nation, which continued to swirl down the
drain. With so many customers, he could probably
run it 24/7, and the parking lots would still stay
constantly full. It was definitely successful, but
he often thought he should sell it and move away to
Chicago or St. Louis where he could have a more
rounded, if not quite so stable and cushy life.
The cushy life part was the real problem; the flow
of cash into the place was addictive. He had been
used to it far too long to even have 'budget'
remain in his vocabulary. The price of success...

Walking through his house, he had a sudden
urge to call Nikki and see how things were going.
They had spent so much time together in the past
two years that he was feeling like there was a
massive hole in his life. But he couldn't call
her. Marcus would probably be home, and there was
no need to go through all the shit they had been
through on the phone the other day. Marcus had
once been his best friend, and now he didn't even
want him to call, or even worse, stop by his house.
There had always been a complexity to the jerk, and
it had only gotten worse in the past two years
since the accident. His behavior had become
nothing less than hostile at best.

Again thinking of Nikki, there seemed to be a
growing bond between her and him again close to the
one they had before she actually married Marcus.
Back then while Marcus had been in residency, they
spent so much time together that he thought maybe
he would marry her. She would have been perfect
for him. They had a lot of common interests and
she used to love to go with him on his buying trips
for the store. The trips had been a lot more fun
with her than they were when he was alone. They
both also seemed to have problems with Marcus, or
at least, that was what she had been saying when he
got to talk to her.

Resigning like usual to eat a cold sandwich
and have a beer, Matt plopped down in front of the
TV for another night. He would watch movies until
he fell asleep in his chair, and later somehow make

50

it to his bed. He now wished he could jump back to
his college days when there were hundreds of things
to do at night. The idea dredged up some good
memories. Maybe he'd head back to the old alma
mater and live it up this weekend. As he finished
his first beer, the thought was briefly tempting.
But after the third beer, he was feeling more
sedate and he decided there wouldn't be anyone he
knew there anymore, and that wouldn't be fun?
University towns were extremely fluid, and the
place he remembered was long gone.

With this thought, he sank further into his
chair and before long, he was absorbed in the
television. With five beers down, drowsiness and
sleep took over. Sleep had always been a restful
experience for Matt. He wasn't an insomniac and he
usually didn't toss and turn. Tonight was a little
different.

After he had been asleep for about an hour and
a half, he began to slowly twitch around in his
chair. At eleven-thirty, he was jarred awake by
the pain in his left hand. What the hell was wrong
with him!

Looking around startled, he saw his lamp in
pieces on the floor. Had he done that? That had
to be why his hand hurt like hell! It had to be
why. And what a dream! He felt like he had been
torn in half! It all seemed so real and it was
still vivid in his mind.

Since the age of fourteen, Matt had been able
to control his dreams, and had learned to enjoy
dreaming. With control over his nightmares, they
faded into oblivion, and he never feared sleep
again. But something was wrong tonight. He
couldn't control this dream no matter how hard he
tried. And he couldn't escape it either. That was
the foundation of his childhood nightmares, and
this had been far worse!

Ray looked up from the checkout counter as
Hedda came into the store. She had been gone for a
long time, so there had to be problems over at the
Lemonte's. They were good kids, and they deserved
to have a good life. But life wasn't always easy.

"Is everything all right, Hedda?" He asked

blank faced.

"Yes, only some little problems that everyone goes through. They'll work through them before long and be O.K.."

"That's good to hear. They're starting out about the same way we did forty years ago. I hope they can manage to avoid the mistakes we made."

"I hope so, too." She said softly. "Maybe we should get together with them and see if you can help me give them a little more advice than what I've been able to give Nikki. I've been mostly listening to her and letting her come to her own conclusions."

"I know you're not the meddling type, but you're right. Why don't you call them and see if they want to come over for dinner this Saturday night? We haven't had them over before, and I think it would be good for all of us."

"You should call, Ray." She said softly. "Nikki might like to hear that you are concerned about what's going on, too. I think it would mean a little more to her."

Easily getting the message, Ray said, "You might be right at that."

A little later, the dinner date was set for the two couples, and since it was closing time, the Krepps started shutting the store down for the night.

Out on the corner under the flickering streetlights, a dark figure stood facing the store. It had an interest in the store, or at least the people inside. A change of thought caused the figure to disappear without any discernible movements, and the darkness left by its absence was a far better thing.

The day turned out to be a killer for Marcus. He was swamped by the backlog of patients from his missed time at the clinic over the past few weeks. The new bump on his head still nagged at him all morning until he finally took some aspirin to kill the pain. He knew he should have told Nikki about the incident in the funeral home, but he had avoided it. She hated the place as much as he did. It would sound foolish anyway, attacked in a shut

down funeral home by who knows what, and then
running away like a scared child. Nothing like
cowardice to make you feel like a real man, he
thought. He hadn't been able to close his eyes
until he passed out from sheer exhaustion this
morning at five o'clock. He could only hope that
his fear wouldn't last through another night...

By the end of the day, Marcus was a nervous
wreck. He needed to get some rest, and the only
way would be to shed his fear of the funeral home.
Before he left work, he called the real estate
agent to check on any possibilities for a sale.
After eight rings, the agency phone was answered in
a rushed and perturbed tone.

"Griggs Real Estate, Janet speaking, may I
help you?"

Knowing that the woman was probably in a hurry
to get home like he was, Marcus tried to be brief.

"This is Dr. Lemonte. Could you tell me if
there has been any interest in my funeral home
lately?"

"Well..uh..let me check, sir," the woman said,
still in a hurried tone.

As Marcus waited for an answer, the dead
silence of 'hold' hit the line. He hated being put
on hold, and it pissed him off to think that she
would be doing anything but looking into his
question. Just as he was about to hang up, the
woman returned to the phone.

"Umm..I'm sorry, sir, but you'll have to call
back on Monday when Norman..I mean Mr. Briggs is
back. I can't find anything myself."

"O.K., I'll do that. Thanks anyway," Marcus
said, hanging up the phone.

The woman's response had been strange when he
asked about the funeral home. He had even heard
something of a giggle out of her when she returned
to the phone. As long as he stayed away from it
another weekend of not knowing whether the place
would sell or not wouldn't kill him.

After locking up his office, Marcus walked out
to his car and climbed in. When the engine refused
to turn over, and there wasn't even a clicking
sound, he decided that his four-year-old battery
had finally given up the ghost. The perfect end to

a perfect week, he thought as he stepped out and started to walk toward home. Halfway down the block, he turned around and walked back to the office. He was too tired to walk all the way home. Nikki would have to come and get him, that's all there was to it.

A few feet from the door, he heard the phone ringing, and had to hurry in to answer it. But just as he grabbed it up, the ringing stopped.

"Hello..hello."

But there was no one on the other end. Just as well, he thought. He was too exhausted to deal with another patient, even if they might be taking their last breath. Quickly dialing his home number, he hoped Nikki would be at the house and able to pick him up. The first ring brought her voice to his ear, and he wasted no time in small talk.

"Nikki, can you pick me up? My battery died and I don't think I can make it if I have to walk back to the house."

"Sure, I'll be there in a few minutes. Do you think you can get a battery tonight so we don't have to worry about it tomorrow? I don't know if I'll be able to get up early enough to take you to the office, and I need my car to do some shopping in the morning."

"Yeah, I might be able to. I'll call a few places before you get here and find out. Be careful coming over here."

It upset her when he said that to her all the time or at least she made him think it did. In fact, it made her feel good. As long as he said that, she knew that he still cared about her.

When Nikki pulled up to the office in the Wisa, Marcus was standing outside with the hood of his car up. At least he was mechanically inclined enough to get the battery out of the car. She doubted he was capable of much else, but he didn't need to be. That's what mechanics were for.

"Did you find a battery?" she asked as she walked up to his car.

"Yeah, the tire place down the street happened to have one by some miracle, and they're bringing it over right now. You can go on home if you want to, and I'll be there in a little while."

"No, that's O.K., I'll wait for you in case you have any more trouble."

"I doubt if I have any trouble with a new battery, but I'm glad you're staying. I could use some hospitable company for a change. It's been one hell of a shitty day, if you want to know the truth."

"I could tell that on the phone. What's gone wrong besides the battery?"

Pausing to decide if he really wanted to dig into his bucket of worms, Marcus finally said, "I wasn't going to say anything to worry you, but my day started yesterday. We can talk about it later when we get home. This isn't really the place for it."

"O.K., we have some other things to talk about tonight anyway. We'll just make it a regular gab session."

Before Marcus had a chance to say anything else, the truck with the battery pulled up beside his car. Ten minutes later, the Lemontes were on their way home, both wondering what the other needed to talk about.

An hour and a half away from Hawthorne in the town of Wellsly, Matt arrived at the home of Terry Blake. Terry had been a good friend of his in college, and he hadn't seen him in over a year. Matt had eventually determined that he needed to be around an old college buddy more than he needed to actually be on the campus. He also needed a change of scenery, and besides, Terry had always had a fascination for dreams. The one he had experienced the night before would surely fire up that old interest.

As Matt knocked at Terry's door, the dream slowly crept back into his thoughts and sent a shiver down his spine. He was going to have to get this one out before it gave him any more trouble. There was no doubt in his mind about that.

"Hey, Matt, how's it goin' man? It's been a long time. If you hadn't come down here, I was thinking I needed to make a trip to Hawthorne to see you pretty soon."

Happy with the warm welcome, Matt relaxed instantly. Good friends were hard to find.

"Yeah, it's been awhile. We need to get together more often. You're only an hour and a half away. Less if I pretend I have a race car." Matt said as Terry let him in.

Laughing, and clearly happy to have some company, Terry took Matt's suitcase and sat it by the door.

"Well, you didn't say much on the phone. I hope you have more to talk about tonight. I thought we would go out, if that's all right with you. There's a decent bar in town that's quiet enough most of the time for talking."

"Sounds good to me, as long as we can talk, I don't mind at all. I have some things or at least one thing in particular that you'll find interesting, I'm pretty sure."

"You're staying tomorrow, too, aren't you?"

"Well, I don't know....Why, did you have something planned? You always were good at keeping busy."

"No, nothing major, just thought we might get away from this town for awhile and have some excitement since we're mostly going to be gabbing tonight."

Hesitating briefly, Matt considered the offer, and said, "I guess I can afford to stay two nights. That is, if you'll let me call my store and tell them I won't be there tomorrow."

"Sure, go ahead. I'll take your suitcase to the spare room and get you a beer."

After a few trivialities innate to friendship, they ate dinner and headed out to the town bar. With both of them happily putting away their second beer, Matt began to tell Terry about his dream.

"You know the weird kind of dream where everything seems real, and when you wake up, you aren't sure it was a dream at all? Well, the one I had last night was like that, and it was the worst nightmare I've had in a long time."

Terry took a slug of beer and settled in to listen.

"The dream started with me walking up a hill

56

along with somebody I didn't know, or at least
didn't recognize from real life. As we climbed up
the hill, it kept getting darker around us, and it
seemed like we would never reach the top. When we
finally did get there, we were looking down into a
deep pit with water at the bottom. We climbed down
into the pit, and as we went further down, we began
to slide. It was then that I realized that the
whole hill was made of bones. As I slid faster
down the bone hill toward the dark water I looked
frantically around, and the unknown person I'd been
with was gone. I couldn't keep from sliding and
just before I slid into the water, I abruptly
stopped somehow. As I lay there trying to fight
down the panic, other things began to move around
me. The still black water began to change as
subtle currents began to slowly move towards me.
As they came closer, I realized that the currents
were the result skulls moving just below the
surface. Still panicking, I turned and tried to
scramble out of the pit, but the bones kept rolling
under my feet and I slid back toward the water
every time I moved. Skeletons crept out of the
water and started clawing at my legs. The next
thing I knew, I finally made it up and out of the
pit. I ran and ran and hopelessly still felt as
though something was chasing me. Then everything
abruptly changed and I was in this little room.
When I looked frantically around, I saw that it
wasn't really a room, but more of a box with
windows on each side but no doors. I had the
sensation that something was outside and was
watching me. I ran to a window and caught a
glimpse of a dark figure as it turned the corner
out of my sight. By this time, I was practically
awake and scared to death. I tried to get out of
the dream, but I couldn't. Something was
definitely wrong. I was trapped in my own sleep.
The black figure I had seen before flew past the
window again, and this time, I could tell it was
shaped like a man that wasn't actually running but
floated above the ground. When I turned from the
window, I felt a sharp knock on my head, and my
whole life flashed before my eyes as I finally
broke free of the dream and woke up sweating and

shaking."

After being caught back up in his dream, Marcus took a few shuddering breaths and went on.

"That was when I noticed my lamp lay shattered on the floor and looked as if it had been smashed by a huge amount of force. The feeling that I wasn't alone carried with me out of the dream, but then it faded away as I tried to clear my head. I tried to convince myself I had knocked over the lamp, but I don't think it should have been possible. I think people in dream sleep are supposed to be rigid in such a way as to prevent them from physically acting out their dreams. I think, I really think that someone was there in my house. That's a big part of the reason I'm here tonight. If something is getting into my house, and is going to attack me every time I go to sleep, I don't think I can live there anymore."

With a look of seriousness on his face that indicated he was no longer pleasantly intoxicated, Terry responded. "I don't know what you want me to do, Matt. I really think you should've called the police. They might have been able to find whoever was in the house. But the dream sounds like a perfectly normal nightmare to me, if you want to call a nightmare normal. I'm sure there's some symbolism in it somewhere, but I can't help you with it when I don't know what's been going on in your life."

"It wasn't perfectly normal!" Matt exclaimed. Nothing has scared me like that since I was a little kid. Do you know what it's like to wake up and know, and I mean really know, that someone was just about to kill you?"

"No, I can't say that I do, but if it's anything like what you've just described, I could happily make it through life without finding out. What do you say to us going back to my house where we can talk about this some more in peace and quiet? I have a lot more beer there."

"What! Are you crazy? I like it right here with people all around us. I'm scared enough right here that I can't imagine going back to your place. You know the saying, 'safety in numbers'."

"Yeah, I guess I see what you mean." Terry

agreed. "I don't think I want to go back there either, now that you mention it. Let's put a few more beers away and try to get this out of our heads, O.K."

Relaxing slightly and waving for the bartender, Matt sat back.

"That's more like it. If we pass out here, we'll be better off anyway. We can talk about this more tomorrow in full daylight."

Three hours later, Matt and Terry were forced to leave as the bar closed for the night. All thoughts of the dream were gone from their plastered minds, so they had no reservations about heading back to Terry's. Even if they had gone somewhere else, it wouldn't have mattered. Nothing happened through the night.

Matt woke the next afternoon with a hangover worse than any in his life. To top it off, it was raining and almost as dark as night. As he crawled miserably from the couch that he couldn't quite remember crashing on, he noticed Terry sitting in a chair on the other side of the room looking worse than he would have if he'd just been shot in the head.

"My god. You look as bad as I feel. What are you doing up so early?" Matt grumbled.

"I feel as bad as you look, too, believe me." Terry returned sickly. "And it's not early...it's already two-thirty in the afternoon, and I've been up ever since your store called to say they needed you back there."

Suddenly tense, Matt yelped, "What! What time was that? Why didn't you wake me up?"

"Slow down, man. I tried to wake you up, but you said to leave you alone or else you'd throw up on me. Believe me, I couldn't handle that and I would have returned the favor. I'm not really much up on that these days. They only called about an hour ago anyway, well, no...it was more like two hours. But I doubt if it was that important anyway."

Still upset, Matt returned to grumbling, "You don't know what incompetent idiots I have working for me back there either, Terry. They've probably blown the store up somehow, and want to know where the stapler is so they can fix it..."

"That bad huh, maybe I should go back with you and kick their butts into shape."

Without hesitating a second, Matt said, "That's a good idea."

"Yeah sure Matt." Terry laughed out.

He had never had a management type job, and wouldn't know what to do if he did. A bachelor's degree in botany just didn't cut it in today's world, and probably never had meant much. He should have taken the teaching route for better job security. Instead, he was now making barely over minimum wage at the local plant nursery, and having to supplement his income with any extra job he could get.

"I'm serious, Terry." Matt said without a hint of humor in his voice.

Trying to understand just what Matt was getting at, Terry kept the smirk on his face just in case the idea was a joke. He knew Matt was always flush with cash, but he had never considered that he could get in on part of it.

"Come on, Matt. You know that I don't have a single business course in my transcripts. And I wasn't raised in the clothing store or anything else even resembling a business." Terry went on.

But having already clearly made up his mind that it was a good idea, Matt kept on encouragingly. "I don't care. You have more intelligence than all of Hawthorne put together, and that's an understatement. Think it over for a few days, and I'll get back to you about it. I've got to get back there now, or else I might end up without a store at all. Not that it would bother me much at this point."

In silence, Terry watched as Matt quickly threw his stuff together, and rushed out the door. He had been serious about the offer; there was no doubt about that. But maybe it was just the nightmare still spooking him. There was no sense in giving the offer any more credit than that.

An hour and a half later, Matt found that the call from the store had been important. His race back to Hawthorne had been stupid, but necessary all the same. The dream analysis would have to

wait until some other time. The nightmare just
hadn't been that bad anyway, as far as he could
remember through the haze of a massive headache. A
dream was a dream and there was no sense in putting
your life on hold while you shivered in your boots.
Especially over something your mind had spun off
after a bad bologna sandwich. It was probably the
last nightmare he would have for another twenty
years anyway.

The thought of having Terry move to town wiped
the dream from his mind. Terry could stay at his
house when he first got into town. He had enough
room, and it would help him keep an eye out for any
prowlers.

Pete wondered what kind of day he was going to
have as he walked out of his house early in the
morning. Things hadn't been very good lately, and
there was no reason for today to be any better.
The life of a paperboy was getting worse all the
time. If only summer would come so that he could
start mowing yards again for a little change of
pace.

Even school hadn't been any fun lately for
some reason. The rest of his life had better not
be like this, or somebody was going to be in
trouble: him. Maybe there would be something new
to do tomorrow.

Jumping on his bike as always, Pete rode off
towards the paper office to pick up his day's work.
He didn't have to wait around for payments today
since everyone had finally paid up. At least there
would be time for him to play ball later on in the
afternoon, or maybe go exploring somewhere.
Thinking about it as the wind whipped past his
face, he decided that was what he would do. He
would go exploring, if he could get Eric to go with
him. He would talk to him first thing at school
and they would probably go exploring.

His paper deliveries and the following school
day drug by like they would never end, and finally
at four o'clock, Pete, Eric, and Harold were on
their way to Chalt Woods. Pete hadn't really
wanted Harold to go because he was a jerk most of
the time. But Eric had told him he wouldn't go

61

unless Harold went. So, Pete knew that he'd just
have to put up with the jerk for the afternoon and
hope that it was fun anyway.

The edginess between Pete and Harold made the
walk to the woods seem longer than it should have.
All three of the boys were tired by the time they
got there, but not one of them would admit it to
the others. It was something of a code that all
boys seemed to follow. Don't let anybody see that
you're tired, or they'll think that you're a weak
little sissy.

"Well, Pete, this was your idea, so what are
we going to do now?" Harold asked just as Pete
knew he would.

Harold was good at making people feel like
worms. Since Harold was a worm, he knew exactly
what it felt like, and tried as hard as he could to
make sure that everyone else did, too. The only
person he left alone most of the time was Eric.
Pete couldn't figure out why they were friends.
Eric wasn't a worm at all, or at least, he didn't
seem to be around him. It really was amazing that
Eric would want to hang around with a jerk that
nobody else liked. Maybe he felt sorry for Harold.
Wormboy sure needed the sympathy.

"What do you want to do, Harold?" Pete asked,
knowing that whatever he would have said would have
been shot down as it came out of his mouth.

"Oh, this is great, Blair. You bring us all
the way out here, and we're not even going to do
anything. What do you think of that, Eric?"

"Lay off, Harold. We came out here to
explore, and you know it. Isn't that right, Pete?"

Feeling relieved that he wasn't alone in this
one, Pete said, "Yeah, that's right. But if you
want to Harold, we can go back and sit in your yard
or something fun like that."

Seeing that he didn't have a comrade to goad
him on, Harold backed down and said, "I didn't say
that. It's just...it's just that I thought you had
some special plans or something, Pete. I don't
want to go home now, do you?"

"Of course not, we came out here to explore,
and that's what we're going to do if it kills us."
Pete said, knowing that he had won that little

battle.

At least he knew that Eric was on his side when it came down to choosing one way or another. That knocked Harold back in his place better than anything else. Two against one was never a fair fight, but when you're dealing with worms, anything counts.

Chalt Woods wasn't as far as it seemed to the boys as they trudged along. In fact, it lay right behind the Lemonte house. Since the funeral home sat next to the Lemonte house, and the woods spread behind both of them, stories had sprung up in the minds of kids through the years about both places. Most of the kids in town had heard the stories, and almost all believed them. In fact, even a few of the adults in town thought that there might be some truth to them, particularly the ones about old mad Portraire dragging people into the funeral home and chopping them up. But most of the people of the town placed the stories on about the same level as children's fairy tales, especially since Portraire had been taken away from town. If there had ever had been any proof, Hawthorne had swallowed it up to protect the interests of its people. The three boys were well aware of the stories, and they made sure that they stayed away from that part of the woods. Dead people with no heads, and skeletons in coffins stayed there, and they didn't like for little kids to be poking around. Harold knew it as well as the others did, and that was why he came up with his mean spirited dare for Pete.

"Pete. I dare you to go the front of the woods and touch the funeral home." He said slyly, as if the other two wouldn't see through his totally transparent scheme.

"We aren't playing truth or dare, Harold." Pete said disgustedly.

"We are now, unless you're chicken."

"I'm not chicken. We aren't playing that game and you know it. Besides, if you're so up on going to the funeral home, why don't you go yourself?"

"You are a chicken, aren't you? I knew it! If somebody would have dared me to go first, I would have gone." Harold spouted self-righteously.

"All right then," Eric said, leveling the

playing field, "I dare you to go with him."

"Now wait a minute. I didn't ever say that I was going." Pete shot out, starting to feel trapped into the situation.

With no one left to dare him, Eric sat down. He knew he had a good thing going here. The other boys were throwing fits about going, and it was fun to just sit back and laugh. He didn't laugh out loud, of course.

"Well, you two had better get going. It's starting to get dark out, and it will only be worse then."

With miserable looks at Eric, Pete and Harold finally gave up and started off toward the front of the woods.

"Wait a minute!" Eric yelled. "You have to bring me back something to prove that you went all of the way to the funeral home."

Needing proof made them feel even worse. Neither one had actually intended on going all of the way to the funeral home, but now they had no choice. This whole deal sucked.

As the sun crept behind a distant hill, the light slowly began to fade, and Eric himself began to get a little jumpy. The time passed in slow motion, and what seemed like two or three hours had only been fifteen minutes. The others had been gone way too long, and he couldn't wait any longer. Darkness had almost totally taken over the woods as Eric got up from the ground, and started to go after Pete and Harold. A twig snapped behind him, and he turned jerkily around.

"Is that you, Pete...Harold?"

But there was no answer, and the sudden stillness sent him running towards the front of the woods not caring if he looked cool anymore.

The BMW made it home all right for Marcus, and it was a good thing that it did. If they were going to talk, his bad mood would send them into an argument faster than anything else. They needed this talk, or he knew they were in for harder times than they had ever seen. Divorce was an ugly word that had always turned his stomach. They weren't going to end up as another statistic, no matter what the circumstances were. Unless of course she had been sleeping with Matt Erickson and that would prove to be another story. If that ever happened, Marcus knew he would end up in prison on a double murder charge. Loving Nikki was one thing, but love had to be a two way street, or there was no sense in even caring at all. He wasn't wrapped around her finger like he used to be, and if she abused him; he didn't really give a shit what happened to her. A flare of anger briefly came with the smell of hotdogs and popcorn, but the smells faded quickly as he asked Nikki, "Well, do you want to eat before we start into this?"

As they walked to the back door and went into the house, Nikki responded, "I think we had better. I've got some chili on the stove, and we can have sandwiches if you want."

His stomach growled at the thought of chili, and the hotdog and popcorn smells faded further away.

"That sounds pretty good. I've been hungry for chili all week."

"I know. You told me about ten times already. I wish that you liked more of the things that I do so it would be easier on me."

"You know that you don't have to fix anything special for me, I'll eat anything that you fix."

"I'm not complaining. I just thought that you'd like one of your favorites so that you'd be in a better mood to talk. That's why I made the chili, and I made enough for you to put in the freezer to eat when you want."

"Thanks, Nik, but you didn't have to do that."

Neither one of them said a word as they sat down to eat. Both were trying to figure out how to say what they needed to say and neither one was ready or willing to open up yet. They drew out the meal as long as they could, and then, after an hour, cleared the table and went to the living room.

"You know, Nikki. I think we really need this talk. We might say things that upset each other, but we have to accept that and realize that it's for the best."

"I'm glad you see it that way, too, Marcus."

Nikki quietly said.

"No, I'm serious, Nikki. I haven't really thought about this before, but every time you say something that I don't like, I get up and walk away from it. I don't even stop to think about what you've said, and a lot of the time you're probably right."

What had been obvious to Nikki throughout there entire relationship was clearly a major revelation to Marcus. Feeling hopeful, she said quickly, "I never have understood why you take off in your car. Don't you realize that driving when you're upset is dangerous? And not just for you, but for everyone else on the road, too."

"Yeah, I know," he started, "but there's something in me that makes me do it. Ever since I first got my driver's license, I've taken off in my car to calm myself down. I think it would be hard to change such an ingrown habit."

Briefly looking into his eyes, she said, "The thing is, Marcus, you're going to have to change if you want to stay alive. I need you to stop doing that because sometime, something bad is going to happen to you. Our lives will be ruined, Marcus. You have to think of the future."

Thinking about the string of seizures he had been assaulted with recently, the plate in his head, and the fact that he had almost died, guilt pulled Marcus down several notches.

"I'm really sorry about that, Nikki. I'll try to keep from doing it anymore. I guess that I just haven't given it much thought before, and I didn't realize that it bothered you so much."

As a momentary pause came to the conversation, and just as he was about to bring up the seizures, they both heard frantic pounding at the back door. With the sounds reverberating through the house, Nikki jumped up and ran to the kitchen.

"Wait for me, Nik." Marcus said as he followed her to the door. "It might be someone needing my help."

His statement having hit a raw nerve, she blurted, "If they need a doctor, Marcus, they can wait until you get to the door. You're only a few feet behind me."

When Nikki opened the door and saw Eric Hopston standing there, his eyes full of tears, she nearly blurted out 'What do you want.' But the kid ran by her babbling something about Pete and Harold, and didn't calm down until Marcus pushed him into a chair and told him to catch his breath.

"Settle down, son. What's wrong? I can't understand you."

"It's Pete...Pete and..and Harold have been eaten..by the skeletons. They haven't come back from the place..." and as his breathing slowed, he explained what had just happened until Marcus finally understood.

Pete and Harold had gone into the woods toward the funeral home, and hadn't come back. It had been a long time, and they hadn't come back!

As Pete's mom looked out her kitchen window, she saw the figure on the corner. She had never seen it there before, but now that it was, she felt something was wrong. She glanced down at her dishes and when she looked up, the dark figure was gone. It made her feel better to see that it was gone. She didn't know why, but it made her feel a hell of a lot better...

CHAPTER 5

The clothing store had Matt trapped into a miserable and mundane life. His only hope for some freedom would be Terry, if Terry decided it was a good option to move to Hawthorne and work at the store. He already knew he couldn't trust anyone in this little town to help with the business. At some points in the past two years, Matt had considered bringing Nikki into the business. But then Marcus actually pulled through by some miracle and his plan died before he even mentioned it to her. Nothing had changed at the store in the mean time. He could barely find clerks skilled enough to unload boxes of clothes and count change. Actually, counting change seemed the major obstacle to employment, when he thought about it. And he

67

had thought about it repeatedly over the time that he had run the store. His life was trickling away by the day, and almost all he had to show for it was the money. Sure, Terry would cut into his profits a little, but it would be well worth it in the long run. He could even extend the store hours some to accommodate the financial loss if he found it necessary.

Sitting at his desk in the back room of the clothing store, Matt listened as two women argued over a dress they had both just found at the same time. Just what he needed, a scuffle, no actually a catfight over a stupid piece of cloth, he would probably end up in a lawsuit over it somehow when the dust cleared. It almost made him wish nudity had come into fashion. But a smile crept onto his face as the two hideously obese arguing women came into his view, and he instantly decided that nothing was as bad as he had just imagined. The only real problem was that they were too busy. Not a problem at all, financially speaking for him. But for the average person just working for the place, any customer could easily be one too many. He would always remember that from the days when he had worked here for his dad. Those dreadful monsters who came in at five minutes 'til closing time 'just to look round'.

His dad had always said, "Just let 'em look, boy. Don't run 'em off. They might just be paying your way through school if they stay here looking long enough."

And he had always remembered those words, as much as he hated then at the time. Every customer was a potential profit, and every one of them had to be treated as if they were buying out the store. As busy as they were now, just his presence in the store gave his people the moral support that they needed to get through the rush. It was nice, in a way, to know that he was needed somewhere.

The rest of the day went quickly, and before long, he was on his way home. He didn't remember the dream from two nights before until he walked in the door and saw the broken lamp on the floor. He should have cleaned that mess up earlier so that it wouldn't be there to remind him of the nightmare

today. Grabbing a broom and a dustpan, he made
quick work of it, and soon he only had his own
thoughts to remind him of the dream.

After all of the events of the day, it was now
late evening and he again had nothing to do. It
would be stupid to drive all of the way back to
Wellsly again just for another drunken night. He
was going to be sitting at home for the millionth
time alone unless some miracle appeared out of the
woodwork.

The evening slowly slipped into night, and
before long, Matt was getting too tired to even
think about doing anything. Whatever he did
though, he couldn't fall asleep in his old chair
again. That in itself might be enough to spur
another nightmare. Not exactly a happy thought for
a tired mind and body. As Matt struggled to stay
awake, he suddenly jumped up and turned the
television off. He had to get out of the house.
He would take a drive. It would shake the sleep
off. He might even stay in a motel to avoid
sleeping at his house for the night. He should
have made the drive again back to Wellsly, but it
was way too late now.

Grabbing his keys, he ran outside. A brief
look at his car as he opened the driver's side door
brought an idea to his cloudy brain. It was about
time for him to get a new car. He had owned this
one longer than he had owned any other car in his
life, and it was definitely time for a change. He
was getting tired of his old rough riding Jaguar
two-seater anyway. It was about time to grow up,
ditch the sporty import, and get a family-type car.
No telling if he would ever need it, but there was
still a chance. Thirty-three wasn't quite over the
hill yet and besides, the solitary life was
starting to get to him. If Nikki would truly open
her eyes to him, they could probably have a good
life together. He would have to get his old buddy
Marcus out of the way though, and that would be a
task! To do that, he would have to work his way
around Marcus until Nikki was able to actually see
that Marcus wasn't the right man for her.

Then there was always the chance that he might
find someone else that he could fall in love with.

That hadn't happened yet, and it was highly unlikely in Hawthorne. Especially since he knew that he wouldn't let it happen. Every girl that he saw only reminded him of Nikki in some way or another. That wouldn't really be fair to the girl, not that fairness mattered when it came to love. One of the two lovers always cared more than the other person was capable of. It was the way of the world; nothing could be fair and equal.

Creeping down the street in his jag, his eyes glanced from house to house admiring the nice ones, and mentally criticizing the ugly ones. This would be a better thing to do on a walk. But he felt secure in a car, especially a moving one. The blocks and the time moved by with infinite slowness, so he was going to have to find a better way to spend the night. He would run out of gas pretty soon anyway, and Hawthorne didn't have an all night gas station. Sometimes this small town got on his nerves. Actually, this small town always got on his nerves. There was nothing to do at night, nothing to do ever if he really thought about it. Why hadn't his father owned a store someplace where there was something to do? Stupid thought, he knew, but it had always bothered him. A forward thinking place with a population twice that of Hawthorn's three thousand would have a dozen more things to do and even one thing was more than Hawthorne had. But then, he didn't have to live here. It was his choice, and if it weren't for the store and maybe Nikki, he wouldn't.

Pete wasn't too happy about the situation he was in. First of all, he hated dares, especially spiteful ones issued by worms like Harold. Being with Harold was another thing. He couldn't stand the guy in the first place, and now they were both off on this miserable dare just because of him. The disgustingness of Harold never ceased to amaze him. The worst thing though was having to go to the old funeral home, with Harold or anyone else. Even having some superhero with him wouldn't comfort him on this horrible trek into fear. And since a slimy old worm was nothing in comparison to a superhero, how was he supposed to get through

70

this? He would though, just to get back at and
torment Harold. After all, Harold had to deal with
the dare the same as he did thanks to Eric.

As they got closer to the front of the woods,
the sky gradually became darker. Maybe it was only
a trick of their eyes, but it was real enough to
make them flinch at every little sound. The
shadows were fading in the decreasing light, which
helped them move along somewhat. But once they
were that scared, there was no way to change it.

At last, they reached the front of the woods,
and they could see the back of the Lemonte house in
the distance. Afraid that the Lemontes might see
them and wonder what they were doing, the boys
stayed in the trees to skirt their yard and moved
off toward the funeral home. With each step that
took them closer, the blackness of its silhouette
gradually filled the sky and eventually sucked away
all the light leaving them with only one thing to
look at. Staring at all of its blackened windows
and unkempt shrubbery, the funeral home ate at
their hearts until fear wasn't just a feeling, but
a part of their very souls. The depth of the
darkened windows gave them the nightmarish feeling
that hands could reach out at any time and rip them
from their lives into the blackness of a thousand
deaths. There would be no escape from this place
if they dared to enter. Eleven-year-old hearts
were strong, but not strong enough to withstand
such an impossible terror.

Pete's eyes wildly scanned the back of the
funeral home for anything that could be easily
taken as proof that they had made it all the way.
Standing as far away from the place as he could,
but at the same time trying to keep close enough to
see if there was anything he could pick up ended up
being impossible. With an incredible effort of
will, he pushed Harold in front of him and followed
him to within a foot of one of the gaping windows.
Both visibly shaking now, they couldn't avoid
looking through the window that was now only inches
from their faces. For a minute, their eyes stared
into pure unyielding darkness. With no warning,
they both let out screams loud enough to deafen a
person blocks away and took off for the road as

fast as they could.

Anyone passing the old funeral home that night would have seen two boys, eyes wider than baseballs, careening down the driveway. It would have been a strange and maybe even humorous sight to a new person in Hawthorne, and long time residents would probably have shrugged it off as the kids' wild imaginations setting them to flight. These people would have all been wrong. The boys' eyes had caught sight of something that was by no means just in their imaginations. People do not walk out of walls!

In the home of realtor Norman Briggs, an unusual discussion was just taking place. A person from some distant town had called minutes before inquiring about the old Lemonte funeral home, and Norman had told them that it had already been sold in the last week.

"What are you talking about, Norman?" his wife asked as he got off the phone.

"That was a minister from over in St. Louis...Wanted to know if the old funeral home was still up for sale."

"I heard that, Norman. But why did you tell him that it'd been sold? You know very well that it's still on the market."

"I know, I know. But it's just not the kind of place that a church would want to be looking into, if you know what I mean. I've had too many weird experiences in that place myself just trying to sell it. There's no telling what other people have experienced there."

"What do you mean spooky stuff? You've never told me anything about that old place. It can't be that bad, can it?"

"Yeah, it's that bad, Phyllis. I don't think that you could handle hearing any of it. You have enough trouble getting to sleep on a normal night, let alone after watching a horror movie. I don't think that it would be fair for me to tell you anything when it's already dark outside."

"Oh, don't treat me like a little kid, Norman. I want to hear what's been happening to you in that place."

Norman knew that he shouldn't say anything more to her though. His wife was one of the biggest gossips in the whole town of Hawthorne. If he told her even a little, the place would never sell. He still had a hefty commission riding on the sale of that place, and he wasn't about to let his wife screw it up for him. He had already gone through enough shit to sell that place forty times. He would probably get rid of it pretty soon if he would be a little less selective and a little more patient. A twang of remorse about turning away the minister caught him harshly in the gut for a second, but then passed. He knew he had done the right thing in that respect. But Phyllis's nagging became too much for him in time though, and he eventually had to tell her a few things just to shut her up.

"Since your life seems to depend on this so much, Phyllis, I guess I'll tell you a few things that have happened to me in that old place. I don't want to hear any more about this afterwards though, and if I find out anything has left this house before that place sells, YOU will be showing the place yourself."

Feeling that she had won another little battle with Norman, Phyllis sat back in her chair to hear what she thought she had wanted to hear just a few minutes earlier.

"As you know, I've shown that place more than forty times since Marcus Lemonte's mother first asked me to sell it almost eight years ago. In the beginning, I didn't have anything out of the ordinary happen to me. But after a few showings, the place started to get to me, and I thought that I had to be imagining things. You know what I mean...footsteps in the rooms overhead, doors closing on the other side of the funeral home, and other things that you can't see but could easily be caused by rats, mice, or even the building settling.

It had always bothered me that Marcus Lemonte's dad had died in that place, and I think maybe that was what started getting to me. It's crazy, but the thought of that one person dying in the place was a lot worse than the fact that the

funeral home had housed thousands of other dead
people over the course of time.

Anyway, one day, I stupidly got there about an
hour before my clients were to show up. I walked
around for a while trying to make sure that
everything was straightened up so that the place
might sell a little easier. When I had finished, I
still had about half an hour to kill. It didn't
feel right to sit in there with nothing to keep me
occupied and distracted. But with nowhere else to
go in such a short amount of time, I stayed and
decided to have a seat on one of the old benches in
the front hall. The benches all face the massive
staircase that rises to the second floor and I
could clearly see all the way to the top. When I
sat down, I couldn't help but feel some relief
after being on my feet all day. I kept looking at
my watch hoping the people would show up early.
The time crept by slower than you could possibly
imagine with me not wanting to be there alone as I
was in the first place. When my clients didn't
show on time, I almost left to call them and move
the appointment to another day. Actually, I did
get up and head for the door, but I stopped after
my first step when I heard a strange pounding noise
coming from the top of the stairs. Reluctantly
turning back around, I vaguely noticed that my butt
had plopped to the floor as the shock of what I was
seeing hit me. Rolling slowly down the stairs was
what looked like a human head, all white and with
hair flopping about wildly. The head thumped to
the bottom of the stairs and slowly rolled up to my
feet. By that point, I guess I was starting to
lose consciousness. The last thing that I can
remember is the head landing upright as its mouth
opened spewing out a sickening yellowish fluid
followed by the most hideous scream I have ever
heard. I swear it could have woken the dead, but
it didn't keep me from passing out.

When I came to, the prospective buyers were
staring down at me like I was a fool. The little
kid that they had with them was giggling and
pointing at me. When I looked down at what he was
laughing at, I realized that I had wet my pants.
That attempted sale didn't quite go through, as you

can imagine."

Phyllis chuckled a little silently and covered it up with her hand finding much more to laugh at than to fear in his story. As ridiculous and pathetic as it was, Norman appeared to be serious. She continued to choke the oncoming laugh down, and let him tell her more.

Going on without pausing as if he wouldn't get it out otherwise, Norman continued. "Then, about two months later, I finally built the courage to go back into the place. This time, however, I thought I was getting the upper hand by taking one of my associates with me. If I was going to see anything else that bad, I wasn't going to be the only one losing control of my bladder. You didn't ever know this either, I'm sure, but I was about ready to check myself into a mental hospital after that first scare, and I was dead serious about it.

Of course, nothing happened with my associate there, and I was having real doubts about myself. I even drove over to the library in Patton to read up on some things of the like I had seen."

Unable to contain herself any longer, Phyllis burst out laughing and jumped out of her chair with the exuberance of a teenager.

"Where are you going, Phyllis?" Norman asked as he watched her trot off toward the kitchen.

"I'm going to call the men in the white suits. I don't think that you tried hard enough to get yourself locked up, but I'll make sure that they take you away!"

Suddenly furious, Norman decided he didn't care if he scared the shit out of her now.

"Damnit, get back in here, Phyllis, this isn't funny! I really did see that and I'm positive I did because I've seen a hell of a lot more than that since then. Do you want to hear about any more of it or not?"

"I don't know, Norman, I might laugh too hard to hear you or maybe laugh so hard I wet my pants. You would understand that wouldn't you." Still laughing she sat back down. "I haven't heard any of these little kiddy ghost stories in years, and I had forgotten how pathetically stupid and childish they were."

"Believe what you want, but I saw what I saw, and nothing can change the way that I feel about that place. Maybe you need to go see a few things yourself, and then you won't have a choice but to believe me."

Continuing to laugh, she boldly said, "Maybe...But I doubt it."

"I'm going to tell you about one other incident, and if you still don't believe me by then, you're going over there to see for yourself."

"Great, now you're throwing idle little threats at me so that I'll believe you. You really are losing it over that place, aren't you?"

"Just listen, Phyllis!" He yelled.

"Well, I.."

"Listen, damnit!"

With the room finally quieted down, he began again, "For the next year or so, I always took someone with me when I went to that place. Occasionally, things would happen, and other people have seen some of them. They haven't dared spread any stories around town though because they know that I'll fire them and have their licenses revoked if they do.

One of these times and just in the past few months, I had my secretary, Janet Portraire, with me. We had a showing that evening with some people from Vincennes, and they weren't supposed to be there until about nine o'clock because of travel time. This was the first time that Janet had gone with me. I guess some of my brokers had let a few things slip, and she had heard some stories about the place. Well, anyway, she had asked if she could go with me this time, and since all of my other people had plans of some kind or another, I agreed.

We were walking around the upstairs of the place and I was having the same queasy feelings that I always had. She had sort of a defiant air about herself that I didn't like too much. It was almost like she was daring the place to do something to her. Believe me, that place doesn't need any encouragement. I thought that her attitude was going to drive the devil himself straight out of hell, the way she was strutting about.

I guess I was pretty relieved when the people actually showed up early to look through the place. We walked around for at least an hour and talked, but I was careful and didn't let on about anything unusual about the place. I really wanted to get rid of it by then. With my experience, I could tell that they weren't interested, but I kept pushing and driving them even further away from a sale. I think that they had to sense that there was something wrong. Within the first few minutes of the showing, their eyes were darting around at every little movement in the shadows. The longer we walked around, the more the tension built up in there. From the past, I could tell that something was about to happen. It only made it worse that Janet really wanted a ghost to reach out and touch her from a hole in the darkness.

We were looking at the last room at the end of the hall upstairs when I felt an ice-cold draft swirl around me and send chills down my spine. That was all the warning I needed. I tried desperately to push the people out the door, but they were frozen in their tracks. The chill had swallowed us all.

The draft intensified, and I could tell that they were all feeling it again by the expressions on their faces. I was really scared by now, and my voice was cracking as I again tried to push the people out the door into the hall.

They were starting to budge a little when I noticed a dark figure in the far corner of the room. I couldn't help but stare, and the others' eyes flew to the same spot.

The figure didn't move at first, but I thought that it was in the dark shadowy form of a person. Janet started walking toward the figure, shrugging my hand off her shoulder as she went. I tried to hold her back, but I couldn't do that and also push the other people out the door.

As I watched in horror, she walked around the old bed in the center of the room and moved into the shadows. The air around me froze as I watched her back out of the shadowy corner and fall onto the bed. The figure that had been in the corner appeared over her out of nowhere, and before she could move, merged into her body and then disappeared.

Janet lay there on the bed, her eyes about to pop out of her head, and began to cry uncontrollably. I heard the pounding of running feet behind me, and turned around half expecting to see a plague of demons.

The people were gone, and I could clearly hear their echoed footsteps from the lower floor as they tried to get out.

I managed to pull Janet off the bed, and practically had to carry her out to the car, by then too afraid to even glance back once. She hasn't gone back there with me since, and she hasn't said a word about what happened that night ever since then. In fact, the whole traumatic experience affected her pretty severely, and she never has quite gotten back to normal."

Stopping, he felt confident in asking her, "Do you believe what I told you now Phyllis, or are you going to have to find out the hard way for yourself?"

In a contemptuous way that made Norman wonder why the hell he had ever married her, Phyllis simply said, "When do we go potty pants?"

The nursing home in Breklettin was as peaceful as always in the early morning. Most of the patients, or residents as they preferred to call themselves, were far into their restless sleep and wouldn't pull out of it until about noon. Age was taking a heavy toll on these people. Most could barely make it to the bathroom on their own anymore let alone step beyond the borders set by the walls of the home.

In the director's office, an intensely serious meeting was taking place concerning the running of the home. The board had come to the conclusion that the current director wasn't fit to run their home, respectable as it was, considering his clearly evident past record in the place. A huge stack of undelivered documents sitting beside his desk was the basis of their argument and the foundation upon which his termination was now being demanded.

"We still can't understand why you never sent out all of these packages here, Frank. We've collected an almost endless series of complaints from relatives, you know." Said the senior board member harshly, "And we have discussed this issue more than once."

"I was getting around to it." The director managed to say.

"Sure, Frank. We can believe that, just like you were getting around to it five years ago when some of these papers first came into your office."

Caught in his own laziness and stupidity, the director laid his head on what used to be his desk and began to cry. His half-assed work ethic had cost him his job finally and it was doubtful that he could get another one in the future because of it.

As the board members started to file out of the office, one of the last to leave glanced around to take a last look at the former director. A wisp of smoke caught his eye, and a second later, flames erupted from the pile of papers.

"Fire!" he screamed, as he pulled the man in front of him back into the office. "Get some water! Hurry!"

Tearing his jacket from his back, he threw it on top of the spreading fire, and shot a shitty look at the director.

"What the hell did you do that for?" He barked. "Your job's already down the tube. Why do you have to screw it up for the next guy?"

"But I didn't do it." whined the director. "I swear, I didn't do it.."

"Like hell you didn't do it! You're the only one in the room who would have a reason to." The board member said as a crowd of others began to surround the director's desk.

Pushing the stack of papers and packages to the floor to spread them out, the board members watched in amazement as one of them instantly began to smoke and caught fire. Before anyone could stomp the flame out, one of them had grabbed it up.

The flame began to eat at his hand and he waved the papers frantically to put it out. A cup of water came flying through the air, followed by a burst of steam as the flame was doused. The director had put the final work of his career into the retirement home. No one was grateful.

Staring at the strange old piece of paper, the men watched as it again began to smolder even while it was wet. Another cascade of water fell from the surrounding area as all of those with cups still in hand contributed to the cause.

"What the hell is that paper?" One of the men choked out as steam continued to pour from it.

Struggling to open the parchment before it again ignited, they looked at each other puzzled when they finally did get it open.

"I can't read anything on this" was the next consensus of the day.

Eagan Portraire hadn't seen fit to translate his message.

"They couldn't have just disappeared, son." Marcus said as he tried to calm Eric down enough to hear the story.

But Eric just kept trying to get them to go outside, and they finally gave in and followed him. He led them straight back to the woods and started to go in, but Marcus grabbed his arm and pulled him back.

"We're not going any further until you tell us what's really going on here. Is it Pete the paperboy who's lost? If you can't explain it to us, we won't know what to do."

"Yes, you have to tell us what's going on here, O.K." Nikki put in, sounding a little more understanding than Marcus.

After a few minutes of continuous coaxing, they finally got Eric to calm down and tell them what had happened. He gave them the whole account of their journey to the woods to explore, of the dares, and of the resulting loss of his friends. Then he started to ramble on hysterically again about the monsters in the woods, and he began shortly afterward to cry again.

"We'll look for them," Marcus said, "and we'll

find them even if it takes the police to do it."

They all looked for the two boys for a few hours until Nikki decided to call their homes and see if they had gone there. By this time, Marcus was searching hesitantly around the old funeral home, and had found the cap that Pete had apparently been wearing when he had ventured where he shouldn't be. The thought that two little boys had been playing around the old place scared the hell out of him. After being knocked on the head in there, or whatever had happened, there was no telling what might happen to two little kids. If something had overpowered him in there it might tear them to shreds and not even exert itself doing it.

When Nikki came over to him with the news that both of the boys were home, and had been babbling incoherently about ghosts, Marcus quickly got away from the funeral home and rushed them all back to the house.

"What's wrong, Marcus? You don't actually think that they saw something in there do you? I mean, they're only little kids, and you know that they can have some pretty wild imaginations."

But she said this without much conviction, and Marcus knew that she was frightened by the thought that there might be something so terrible in the funeral home. He would have to tell her what had happened to him the other night.

"After we run Eric home, we need to finish our talk from earlier, Nik." Marcus said softly.

Having heard that the other two boys had seen ghosts, Eric hung closely to Nikki and Marcus as they walked over to the car. He would have to call Pete and Harold when he got home to find out what had happened to them. If it had anything to do with ghosts though, maybe he had better wait until morning to find out. That was what he needed to do, wait until it was fully light outside to hear what had happened. He knew one thing for sure though. He wasn't ever going out into the woods again, and he especially wouldn't go anywhere near the old funeral home.

On the way to Eric's house, Marcus drove past the funeral home even though it was out of the way.

The place sure as hell was creepy. He hadn't ever really thought about it back when he went there with his dad. The long drive that was very uncommon for a funeral home, the old trees that lined the drive and made an intensely dark tunnel as they overlapped it, and all of the blackened windows which gave it the appearance of having a multitude of eyes keeping constant watch, it was no wonder no one wanted to buy the place. He sure as hell wouldn't.

"You haven't ever been close to that old place have you Eric?" Marcus asked, seeing Nikki give him a dirty look.

"No. I hear all kinds of stories about it, and I'm afraid to go there. I couldn't believe that Pete and Harold went, even if it was a dare."

"Well, I want you to make me a promise. I don't want you or any of your friends to go anywhere near there ever again, O.K."

With a shrug of acknowledgment, Eric agreed to his request, and soon they were pulling into his driveway.

"Thanks for bringing me home. Can I have Pete's hat so I can give it to him tomorrow?"

"Well, I thought that I might give it to him tomorrow myself when he delivers our paper."

"Oh...I guess that would be O.K." Eric said, a little disappointed that he didn't have a reason to go see Pete the next day. He would go anyway, of course. But that would have been a good excuse to go over tonight, and maybe even get to spend the night.

"Bye, Eric, and remember what I said, O.K."

And with that, Nikki and Marcus drove off. They were both quiet on the way home, and it didn't look like they were going to talk anymore at all that night when Nikki finally spoke up.

"You shouldn't scare those kids anymore than they already are. I don't know if there's any truth to their story, but I don't like that place for my own reasons, and we don't need any more stories drifting around if we're gonna ever get rid of it."

"I know that, Nikki, but I just don't want anybody getting hurt over there. I haven't told

you this, but I was over there the other evening
after we had that fight, and something happened to
me."

What! Why didn't you tell me!"

"I was afraid that night, and I didn't want to
bring it up and scare myself anymore. I didn't
think that you needed a scare that night either,
Nik. But if you want to know now, I'll tell you."

"You're going to have to start telling me
things when they happen, Marcus. Otherwise, I'm
going to worry even more every time you leave the
house."

After a short pause, Marcus began.

"Well, you know why I left in the first place.
When I took off, I was going to go on one of my
drives, but it just didn't feel right that day. It
didn't seem like it was going to do any good, so I
turned around and drove back.

As I was going past the funeral home, I had
this sudden urge to pull in. The next thing I
knew, I was opening the back door. I sensed
something strange there, and it started to get at
me before I even touched the door handle, so I
turned around to leave. Just as I got to my car,
though, I saw a flash of light come from one of the
funeral home windows. I thought someone had broken
in, so against my better judgment, I went back to
see who was trying to rob the place. There are
still a few things in there worth a little money,
you know, and I couldn't see losing them to some
thief.

It was really dark, so I tripped around in the
back room for a while before I made it to the
hallway. Bringing it down to the basics, I've
never been so afraid in all my life. When I
started to go down the hall, I felt a presence of
some kind that seemed to surround me. There was
also a harsh chill that kept swirling around the
hall, but I figured that it must be due to the back
door being open. But then the presence seemed to
get stronger, as if it knew that I wasn't going to
turn around and leave. The air became so heavy and
oppressive that I thought I was going to choke to
death. Maybe it was just my imagination, but when
I was about to pass out, I thought I heard

footsteps. When I hit the ground, the last thing I think I saw was a dark figure looming over me.

I don't know how long I was out. You probably can figure that out better than I can because I don't know what time I left or what time I came home. When I did wake up, I had a tremendous headache. There was a bump on my head the size of a golf ball that was either due to me being hit, or was the result of me being slammed to the floor. I kind of like to think that it was from a person swinging a bat, because that would rule out any of the other things that have filled my imagination since then.

Anyway, when I woke up, the choking sensation was gone, and I got up and ran out of there as fast as I could move without literally tearing through a wall.

When I drove away from the funeral home just to come next door, I felt a thousand times better. But feeling better wasn't enough to make me capable of telling you that night. If you remember, I went straight to bed, even though I didn't sleep the entire night. I heard every sound that filtered into our bedroom that night as footsteps, and every shadow looked like it was going to attack me.

Do you see why I warned the little kid to stay away from there now? If another person died in that place, I think that I would probably have a breakdown. There is something seriously wrong with that place, and I'm almost ready to burn it down to prevent it from hurting anyone else."

The car was swallowed by silence as Nikki tried to take in Marcus's story. To think that someone almost killed her husband, and she hadn't even known about it. Her gut feelings that day had been sickeningly valid. It was bad enough that he hadn't told her, but she now knew it wouldn't matter anyway because her gut would tell her, and she couldn't imagine how she would handle that kind of torment.

The fallout of these thoughts was a flood of tears flowing from her eyes, and she reached over to hug him knowing that she had come close to losing him forever. Her talk would have to wait. It seemed insignificant now, and upsetting him

anymore would be pretty despicable. She loved him
and didn't want to lose him. That was all that
mattered.

CHAPTER 6

The dark hallway of the funeral home gleamed
with some even deeper blackness as the figure at
the end beckoned Pete to come forward. Against his
will, but somehow compelled to do so, Pete obeyed.
As he went further, each step was like another nail
being driven into his coffin. He knew that when he
reached the end of the hall, he would die. He had
no doubt about it. He desperately tried to fight
the pull.

"NO! I won't come to you! You can't have me.
You can't have me!" But the words that Pete yelled
were of no use. He had no control of his body.
Only his mind was free to fight the pull of the
figure.

Suddenly, from the dark hole of one of the
doorways at his side, a white disfigured hand
clawed at his arm leaving a horrible gash down to
the bone. Blood gushed from the open wound, and
Pete let out a scream of pain, but no sound escaped
from his mouth. There was no hope. His life was
over. He was only a little boy, and his life was
over… This couldn't be happening to him. He had
gone to his room a little while ago, so how did he
get into the funeral home. As the blood poured
from his arm to the floor, he slowly remembered
what had happened. He had gone back to the funeral
home to find his hat. He had to have his hat back,
and that was why he was here now. But something
had pulled his body inside, and, as much as he
fought it, he was here now. All hope was lost. He
was here, and he was about to die. The gleam of
the figures eyes submerged in the darkness made his
heart burn with rage.

The floor unexpectedly gave way, and he was
falling....falling into the blackness that could be
nothing short of hell. Everything was happening so
quickly, as if he was in a dream, a dream that he

couldn't get out of.

And then something had a hold of his shoulder. He forced himself to turn around, and with a scream that woke half of his neighborhood up, he was awake, drenched with sweat, but awake and in his own bed.

Faster than normally possible, Pete ran to his mom's room and jumped into her bed. She hadn't even woken to his screams, and he felt this meant he was now free of danger. Safe.....until he fell asleep.

Across town, Harold was also having horrifying nightmares. The dreams were of demons walking out of walls and chasing him through an endless maze of hallways. The hallways all led to more demons, and when he thrashed himself awake, he was cowering down on the floor next to his bed. The absolute darkness he saw under his bed sent him flying into his parent's room. Shivering, he realized his own house wasn't even safe from the monsters he had seen in the funeral home. He spent the rest of the night awake, afraid for his life.

The day was an incredibly beautiful one for Hawthorne. But Hawthorne wasn't the place to buy a car, or at least not a car that was worth driving. Matt left his house with this thought, but he also knew that he had better check up on the few car lots in town. His dad had built up good relationships with the few dealers here, and he should at least give them a fair shake for the sake of business.

Since the lots were all on the way out of town, the stops were quick, and he didn't waste much of the day in making them. The last time he had gone car shopping, he had found exactly what he wanted at the time in Patton. Patton wasn't even close to being a large city, but the people there did have better car sense. It wasn't far to go either.

On his way out of town, he had to pass Marcus's office, and with some luck he thought had run dry, Nikki happened to be leaving there. Pulling over to the curb, he swung himself out of the Jaguar, and went over to her before she climbed into her own car.

"How are you doing, Nikki? I haven't been able to talk to you for a little while."

"Well, Matt, Marcus and I have been having a few problems. We've been trying to work them out, you know, and I haven't had time to do much outside the house."

"Oh really, that's too bad. I hope you got things worked out," he said without any feeling.

With a shining smile appearing instantly on her face, she said, "I'd say we're close to it, Matt. At least I think it will be easier now. I had some tests done this week, and we got some great news today. About seven months from now, we're going to have the start of the family that we've been wanting for the past few years. Isn't that great! I've never seen Marcus so happy."

"Yeah....yeah that's great, Nikki. I'm really happy for you." He said, but his words came out with a hint of bitterness that he couldn't suppress, and he knew Nikki had noticed.

"Are you O.K., Matt? You don't seem too happy this morning. Nothing's bothering you that I could help with is there?"

"No," he said sullenly. "There's nothing really. I guess I'm just not feeling very good, now that I think about it. I was on my way out of town, but I think I'll just go back home and rest up."

"That's too bad, Matt. Maybe you should have Marcus take a quick look at you. I'm sure he wouldn't mind."

"No, no. I don't feel that bad. I think it's just a cold."

"O.K. then, I'll see you later. I've got to get home myself. I thought I would fix something special for lunch to kind of celebrate."

And with that, Nikki was gone. Matt stood there with an emptiness in his stomach that was not sickness, but was as close to it emotionally as a person could get. He was going to have to go home and do some heavy drinking to put this out of his mind. This had turned into a real shitty day.

Pete woke up with a start as the last of his

dreams finally pushed him farther than he could stand. Nights like that were enough to destroy even an adult's day, but he was determined to plow through this one anyway. The paper route might even be a blessing for a change.

Walking into the kitchen, he got exactly what he expected from his mom.

"What was wrong with you last night, Peter? You haven't had to sleep with me for over four years, and then you about scared the daylights out of me last night when you came diving into my bed."

"Just a bad dream mom, I didn't think I woke you."

"I would say it was more than that by the way you squirmed around last night. I don't think I got any more sleep than you did. As a matter of fact, I know I didn't."

"It was nothing, mom, really!"

"Well, whatever you say, Pete. But I think that you're holding back on me. You know if you have trouble of any kind, you can come to me."

"I know."

But he was out the door and off on his bike before she could say anything else. She wouldn't understand what he had seen the evening before. And because of this, his dreams would be meaningless to her, too.

The paper office was the usual early morning bustle of paperboys, and Pete was glad to see something ordinary and familiar. The day would go fast, now that he dreaded the thought of falling asleep that night. He had even lost his favorite cap somehow, and it made the whole situation worse. Now he didn't have anything left in the world to remember his dad by. He should have quit wearing it when his dad died, but it was a comfort to just be in contact with something that his dad had given him. Now it was gone forever...

Luckily, no one had heard about the events the day before. The other paperboys treated him just like they always did, and he got away from there as fast as he could. When he got down the block though, he slowed down. His route was going to have to be drawn out as long as he could make it. And with any luck, someone would ask him to spend

the night tonight. Staying awake all night would
be easier that way.

But no matter how he tried to avoid it, time
went on as it always did, and soon he was almost
through his route. To make the run slower, he had
been placing each paper on the steps of the houses
by hand, and as he did this at the Lemonte house,
Marcus stepped out on the porch.

"Glad to see that you're alive there, Pete.
We had quite a scare last night when your friend
came running up to the house."

"What!"

"Didn't your friend talk to you last night
some time?"

"No...he didn't..what are you talking about?
How do you know about it?"

"I guess I had better fill you in on what I
know. But first, you had better tell me your part
of the story. Can you come in for a while? I have
something in here for you."

With some hesitation, Pete walked with Marcus
into the Lemonte's house and straight through to
the kitchen. Sitting down at the table, Marcus
finally got Pete to tell him what had gone on the
night before. By the end of it, Pete's voice was
shaking so much he could barely talk.

"Just a second, Pete, and I'll be back. I
have to get something for you."

His throat dry, he managed to get out, "O.K.
But can I have a drink of water before you go?"

"Sure. I'll do even better than that. Would
you like a soda or something instead?"

"That would be fine, Dr. Lemonte."

"How about just calling me Marcus, I don't
like the formality, and I think we know each other
well enough now for that."

"O.K., thanks for the soda, Marcus!"

With that, Marcus made his way to the bedroom
on the first floor and soon came back with Pete's
cap. Pete's reaction on seeing his cap was a
dramatic shift from the miserable and shaking kid
who had just been there. After hearing what the
boy had just told him, he was briefly happy to see
the change. Explaining how it had come into his
hands, Marcus was glad that Nikki wasn't there so

he could drive a little more fear of the funeral home into the boy. The kids had to stay away from the place for their own good just like he did. Soon he was finished, and Pete left with mixed feelings of terror and happiness. One thing was pretty certain. He was going to take Marcus's advice and stay away from the funeral home from now on.

Foolishness was Harold's 'MO' most of the time, and the scare the night before had done little to change it. Waking up that morning and feeling the encouragement of the daylight, he felt the need to go back to the funeral home to see what else might happen. He wanted someone to go with him though, and the only chance he had for that would be Eric.

With a quick phone call, he heard that Eric had gone with his dad to Patton for the day, and wouldn't be home until later that evening. Only a little disheartened by this, he was determined to go as soon as Eric got back, if he could. He spent the rest of the day planning out what he was going to do that night, with or without Eric. He wasn't going to be a chicken like he was the night before. But then, that little wimp, Pete, brought all that on. If he hadn't started running away and spooked the living daylights out of him, he would probably still be there getting rid of those ghosts. As he thought about it, he knew he would have to take along a flashlight, and his old skeleton key. The key might not work, but it would be worth a try. Getting into the place was something he would have to do to get rid of those things that had walked through the wall last night. Thinking about it more, a quick rush of ways to kill monsters raced through his head. What was it that you had to use to get rid of a ghost? There had to be something that he could use.

The list seemed endless: wooden stakes for vampires, silver bullets for werewolves, salted, sewn-up mouths for zombies, and a dozen more. But he couldn't think of anything that would get rid of a ghost. Maybe he would have to think of something new. Soon he was rummaging around in his garage for anything that looked like it might destroy a ghost, or whatever else was in that old funeral home.

After looking for what seemed like hours in his garage, Harold eventually moved to the attic and came across a large, old wooden crucifix. It probably wouldn't do a thing for him, but it was better than nothing in this case. He needed at least one more thing to round out his defense kit. Maybe, when he talked to Eric, he would have a better idea of what they needed to take.

By this time, it was evening, and he tried to get a hold of Eric once more without luck. Eric had better hurry up and get home, or else he was going to have to go alone. When he came to school the next time with his story of triumph, Eric would regret not having been there with him.

An hour later, Eric still hadn't made it home, and Harold was on his way to the funeral home, crucifix in hand. The only thoughts that raced through his mind were "I'll show that wimp, Pete. Eric will regret not being home."

By seven-thirty, a total, moonless darkness surrounded Harold as he made his way up the long drive to the funeral home. The slight breeze that blew through the trees over his head gave him a chill as if warning him of what was soon to come. He ignored it and pushed on. The only thing that he could think about now was that he was about to have proof of his bravery and Pete's weakness.

From behind, Harold heard the sound of an approaching car, and made a dive into the ditch beside the drive so he wouldn't be seen. The people passed on Restview Way without noticing him, and he was soon up and running the rest of the way to the funeral home.

As he walked below the blackened front windows, Harold had the sensation that he was being watched, but again ignored his own limited sensibility. Turning the corner, he approached the nearest side window. He would have to try to get in here. The skeleton key might work in the front door, but he was afraid to be seen from the road of all things. Breaking through the window would add more adventure to the night anyway.

After struggling with the window for a while, just in case it was unlatched, he finally gave up and threw a rock at the glass. Shards flew in all directions, and the noise tweaked his nerves and unsettled his stomach. He climbed up into the blackness, and felt a trickle of blood slide down his arm from a small cut after he hit the floor. Just another trophy added to his brave night.

The smell of the musty room filled his nose as he tried to adjust to the dim light. This might turn out to be a little scarier than he had expected. All of the furniture was draped with old sheets, now rustling slightly with the air drifting through the broken window. He couldn't see much else as he walked deeper into the room, and he soon lost sight of the window.

Against his will, Norman realized that the only way he could get Phyllis off the subject of the funeral home was to take her there. In the short span of time since he had told her the stories, she had already driven the subject into the ground. He knew he wouldn't be able to take much more of her ridicule. But then, with a little luck, something might happen to the bitch, and he could be rid of her ridicule forever.

Phyllis's constant nagging had pushed him into the arms of Janet years ago. If Phyllis was out of the way, he knew he could be a happy man again. Janet had become everything to him. Not only was she beautiful in comparison to Phyllis, but they also shared a lot of common interests. Janet enjoyed the outdoors. Phyllis, on the other hand, took up stupid busybody hobbies like ceramics and weaving. He wasn't the type who could sit inside all day. He needed to be out and about in the open air where he felt healthy.

Thinking about it, he wished there could be some way to insure that whatever was in the old place would come out and blast Phyllis to hell with its full fury. Too bad she didn't have a heart condition. Somehow, reclusive as she was, Phyllis was one of the healthiest people he had ever had the displeasure to know, rolls of fat and all.

"What do you think about me giving Phyllis a

tour of the funeral home tonight, honey?" Norman asked Janet as they lay in the hide-a-bed he had put in his office a year earlier.

"After what happened a few months ago, I don't want you going in there, Norman. But then, you know what I think of your wife. If she accidentally doesn't make it back out, I'll be the first one to clap. You'd be all mine."

With that, Norman gave her a big kiss, and they melted together into the passion that Phyllis had never been capable of. They played at each other's ecstasy for another hour and a half until the office phone abruptly jarred them from their pleasures. He knew immediately that it was Phyllis, and he felt a twinge of disgust.

"Norman," Phyllis's voice barked, destroying the little good feeling that he had left in him, "why aren't you home? You know that I always have your supper ready early on this night so we can go play bingo in Patton."

"I was just getting some paperwork caught up, dear. I'll be home soon though, O.K. By the way, why don't we skip bingo tonight."

"What Norman! You know I look forward to bingo all week. What's wrong with you!"

"Take it easy, Phyllis. I thought we would take that trip to the funeral home you've been bugging me about. It might be kind of fun, you know."

He said this with a smile on his face, knowing that she would like nothing more than to scoff at him. She didn't believe in ghosts, and proving him a fool would delight her to no end. She was definitely a bitch.

"Oh, all right, Norman. I guess we could miss bingo just this once. A change might do us both some good."

And she was off the phone. Norman only hoped that he would gain something worthwhile from the night's escapade. Her demise would definitely brighten his life.

"I guess I have to get home now, Janet. Phyllis is about to have a fit. We might just scare some life out of her tonight, though. I'm taking her to the funeral home."

"You be careful there, Norman. The way things are, I don't want you freaking out and getting killed or something. She's such a nag, I don't think the devil himself could put her in her grave, let alone tolerate her if he did."

"I guess you're probably right. But I have to do it to get her off my back for a while. If nothing else, maybe she'll learn that my imagination doesn't just run away with me every time I walk into that place."

With a last kiss, Norman left Janet to head back to his own personal Medusa. The worn look of a miserable and badgered husband returned to his face, and he was home too soon for his own liking.

"It's about time you got here, Norman. I've been worried sick."

But Norman knew this was about as much bullshit as could be found in any stockyard. She never ceased to amaze him.

"I'll eat and take a quick shower, dear. Then we'll be off to the funeral home."

"Well, hurry up. I want to get this over with by morning. And don't forget to put on a diaper so you don't soil your pants later." She cackled at his back as he headed out of the room. "Better make it super absorbent, too."

He ignored her final shot and forty rushed minutes later, they were on their way to the funeral home. They would be getting there just after dark. He prayed they would see something...something really monstrous.

CHAPTER 7

Marcus and Nikki had an incredible lunch. The news of Nikki's pregnancy had put them both in better spirits than they had been in for a long time. There would probably be no reason to fight with a baby on the way. It was incredible what a baby could do for a marriage, especially before it was born.

That afternoon, much of the discussion revolved around which room would become the nursery

in the Lemonte house. It was really a simple
matter, but how it would be set up was not, at
least, not for them as new parents.

By evening, both Nikki and Marcus were ready
to go to the Krepps, and the thought of a pleasant
visit with the older couple made them feel even
more secure in the idea of a long lasting marriage.
Although times had changed, the possibility of a
long-term commitment holding out was something that
both of them strongly desired. It was too easy to
just give up on something that could be as fragile
as a marriage, and never try to gain back what was
lost.

"Well Marcus, are you about ready to go over
to the Krepp's? They said they wanted us there at
seven, or somewhere around that time." Nikki said
as she walked out of the bathroom, finished with
her necessary tasks.

"Almost, I didn't think that you'd be ready so
fast. Are you sure that you're feeling all right?
I've never seen you get ready this fast."

"I guess it's just the excitement. We're
finally going to have something to show the world
as proof of our love for each other."

"I've never thought of it in those terms, but
I guess you're right. People might have trouble
seeing that we really love each other sometimes.
But then, who really cares what anyone else thinks,
right?"

But Nikki wasn't listening. She had floated
off on one of the many clouds that she had been
riding all day. Her relationship had taken a
sudden upswing, and there wasn't a soul in the
world that could have been happier. As she stared
smiling out the bedroom window, the headlights of a
car pulling into the funeral home driveway caught
her attention for a moment. But she blocked out
the thought of the place and what might be going on
over there as quickly as the car was out of sight.
The thought of someone being there tonight was
ridiculous and didn't stick with her long enough to
tell Marcus about it. Soon he was ready, and they
were out the door to the Krepps. Bad thoughts were
far from their minds.

Shortly later, they pulled up to the Krepp's

95

quiet house on the outskirts of Hawthorne, and Marcus and Nikki locked hands and walked to the front door. After a knock and a quick kiss, they entered the Krepp's home under the twinkling eye of Ray, who led them to the living room where Hedda was sitting.

"Promptness befits a doctor, Marcus, and I'm glad to see that you're still meeting up to my expectations." Hedda said as Marcus and Nikki took seats almost on top of each other.

"I told them you'd say that as I let them in. I hope you kids are hungry. Hedda's cooked up enough food to feed the whole town."

"I know I'm starved, Ray. And Nikki needs to keep her energy up for the next few months."

"Marcus! You shouldn't have told them that way."

"What's this? If you're pregnant Nikki, it's the best thing I've heard in years." Ray said with enthusiasm that couldn't have been matched by anyone but Marcus under the circumstances.

"This is great news you two! We couldn't be happier for you." Hedda said, adding to the excitement. "It almost makes me want to have children again."

For twenty more minutes, the four rambled on about the future addition to the Lemonte household. It was a good beginning for what was to become an even better night at the Krepps. Everything they did and talked about gleamed with a hint of happiness.

At about eleven-thirty as the evening was dying down, Hedda brought up her concern about their recent arguments, but even this didn't dampen the spirits of the evening.

"I honestly don't think we'll have any more trouble now, Hedda." Nikki said with as much assurance in her voice as Marcus had ever heard.

"No, I think we were both being a little childish. We're going to have to grow up now, and make this marriage work."

"It doesn't have to be perfect, Marcus. Just keep your heads clear, and don't let the little things get you down. Ray and I have had out troubles, too, and there's always a way around them, if you're wise enough to see it."

"I couldn't have said it better myself," Ray said, "it just takes a little work sometimes, but in the long run, you'll be glad you made the effort."

The evening over at the Krepps, Marcus and Nikki made their way to their car leaving a trail of "thank yous" behind them. Today seemed like it was going to be the beginning of new and happier times for them, and they believed they deserved it after what they had been through. Too much trouble had developed in their marriage for it to be left unchecked. Now, they had new hope in the form of the coming baby, and with the extra support of the Krepps, all of the forces of hell weren't going to be able to hold them back.

Still drinking that night at nine after having started with Nikki's news that morning, Matt was within a few beers of passing out. The world had pulled a quick flip-flop on him that would only be remedied by a long run of drunken days and nights. With any luck, she had only been joking around, and there would still be hope for him. Luck wasn't one of his bigger fans in life.

Making his way slowly to the bathroom, Matt didn't know whether he should, piss or puke. A sudden heave later and the choice was taken out of his hands. This wouldn't stop him though. He still had a full case left in his refrigerator, and he planned to down it by morning. After rinsing his mouth out with part of a beer, he returned to the kitchen and his growing pyramid of empty beer cans.

But as the minutes crept by, Matt felt his head falling toward the table. No matter how hard he fought it, he was soon snoring loudly. But either a bad dream, or another surge in his stomach brought him abruptly awake, and he stood up to feel his head swirling faster than vomited beer down his toilet bowl.

Stumbling to his medicine cabinet, he found the bottle of amphetamines he had gotten from Terry and popped a couple down. Calling them amphetamines instead of speed seemed stupid and he

97

started to laugh. A big mistake, he soon found, and a sad waste of the pills as they shot out of his throat and into the sink along with some beer that was starting to taste like acid. Being careful not to think about it this time, he took two more pills and made his way into his living room to wait for the effects.

"Too slow" he drunkenly thought five minutes later, and went back for a couple more. He would have to talk to Terry about this bad speed. You just couldn't trust people once you got out of college, not even your best friends. He still didn't feel any effects, but he gradually forgot about it as his thoughts drifted to Nikki. He would have to figure out a way to get her away from Marcus, an idea he had discarded quicker than his first six-pack when he had still been almost sober. But nearing the point of alcohol poisoning, nothing really seemed unreasonable to him now, not even murder.

"Do you think the kids' marriage is going to hold out, Hedda?" Ray asked as Marcus and Nikki pulled away from their house.

"Don't be absurd, Ray! Of course it will. You know how I am anyway. If the slightest problem comes along with that child on the way, I'll be over there to help patch it up before you know I'm gone."

"I guess you're right."

"There's no guessing to it. Those kids don't need to go through what we've been through. We're lucky that we're still married now, and we both know it. Not that it bothers me. I think I'm happier now than I've ever been and I hope you are too."

"Now you're being absurd. You know I'm happy. I didn't ever want a divorce in the first place, if you recall. I was only riding along with what you wanted, even though it wasn't what I wanted."

Continuing to talk as they cleaned up the kitchen from the evening's meal, the two began to recall the good times of their marriage, letting the bad ones fall away. Before long, they were making their way into the bedroom, too tired to

think of much more than sleep. Tomorrow, they
could sleep late, and they had looked forward to it
all week. They didn't have to start their days at
the store so early, but they always did. It was
the way an old corner store should be run. A
tradition they were proud of.

As dreams crept gradually into Hedda's sleep,
a strange, somehow familiar scene drifted before
her eyes. She had been there before, hundreds of
times. Why did it look so different this time?
Was it the mist lying low to the ground, engulfing
the stones? Everything was just too hazy.

In the distance, faint glows of light bobbed
their way toward her. It was good that she was
hidden behind this row of trees so she wouldn't be
seen.

The trees had always been a wonder to her,
enclosing the cemetery into its own little world.
Trips there with her father hadn't been scary at
all. In fact, she had grown to enjoy being there
while her father mowed and dug the occasional
grave.

But now, something was very different about
the place. The mist had never been here before.
Not only that, but it was dark and glows of light
were bobbing slowly towards her. She had never
been here at night, and she didn't want to be here
now.

As she stared through the trees into the
cemetery, the mist began to swirl in places.
Almost instantaneously, huge eyes formed out of the
swirls in the mist. With a stare that should have
driven her crazy, the eyes directed their vigilance
toward her. Fear crawled deeply into her soul.
The lights were getting closer, and the eyes were
going to give her away! There were no doubts in
her mind about that.

The glows that had been on the other side of
the cemetery were now popping up over the nearest
hill. She saw that they were candle flames and the
candles were being held by a procession of hooded
figures. There were more than she could count, and
they slowly surrounded a huge, flat-topped stone no
more than twenty feet from her. She watched as
each figure placed its candle on the stone making

99

it glow strangely in the misty darkness.

Confusion began to overtake her as the intensity of the eyes' glare increased on her. As she let out a small gasp, the hooded figures suddenly noticed the eyes. The eyes floated to her location among the trees and revolved about her, increasing her panic. Her worst fear quickly came to fruition. The figures glided toward her, flashes of jagged steel emerging from their vestments.

She froze as the figures closed in on her. The lead figure's hood slid to its shoulders and she screamed desperately as the horror of realization struck her. The rotting face of her long dead father was the last monstrous thing she saw as Ray woke her from her nightmare.

"This place doesn't look so bad, Norman." Phyllis said spitefully as they drove up to the back door of the funeral home.

"Looks can be deceiving, my dear. I don't want to make this any worse for you than it can be." He said, barely able to hold back the sarcasm.

"I still think you're crazy, Norman. Nothing that you've told me could have possibly happened."

"Give it time, Phyllis. Give it time."

With this, the two became silent as they stepped from the car and walked to the door. Fumbling with his keys, Norman reluctantly found the one he had grown to dread using. How many times had he dropped it as his hand shook unlocking the door? "TOO many", he thought.

The door opened as easily as if someone had pulled it from within. It wasn't the type of thing Norman liked to think about when he had to go into the place. Maybe his imagination was just a little too wild. But then the smell of the prep room hit his nose bringing with it a flashback of his past experiences. Imagination couldn't account for everything. It was ridiculous to even consider it.

With familiarity he wished he didn't have, he maneuvered his way through the room pulling Phyllis awkwardly behind him. He would make sure she regretted this if it was the last thing he did.

With that thought, a touch of raw and irrational
courage warmed his blood causing him to tighten his
grip on her wrist. He could feel the air flowing
around them in cold invisible swirls, and a tremor
from Phyllis's arm gently shook his hand. A little
demeaning would be good for her soul, if she even
had one. But then, it would take more than that to
turn this witch around.

It had to be seven-thirty by now, he
estimated. The rooms were already dark enough to
make a flashlight useful. A flashlight they didn't
have. Phyllis's glowing red pig eyes might be
enough to get them around. They sure lit up the
bedroom at night when he made it in late. It was a
wonder their whole house didn't glow.

Passing a room on the right side of the
corridor, Norman heard a small thump. It was just
a small thing in here, and definitely not enough to
scare Phyllis. She needed something big...really
big, or she'd never back down. At least that was
the front she was still trying to put on. Every
time he'd looked back at her, she had given him a
"well, where are the monsters, bozo" look that made
him want to shove a pitchfork in her glowing eyes.

With that thought in mind, he pushed through
the door leading to the massive front room and felt
a slight chill rush down his spine as he caught
sight of the staircase. He really hated this
place. There was no way to convince him otherwise.
The thought of that head rolling down those stairs
almost made him turn tail and run. But Phyllis's
arm in his hand reminded him of his purpose. He
would shake hands with the devil himself to put her
in her place. And then, sometime in the near
future he would have Janet without having to hide
it from the old bat.

Feeling a shove at his back, Norman went on
into the front room. How could she be so eager to
do this? She was the crazy one, for sure, and she
didn't seem to be satisfied with her own insanity.
She was out to push him over the edge, too.

Even Phyllis's steps slowed as the air
seriously chilled around them. Somehow, the
coldness of the air made the room seem even darker,
and shadows leapt to life in the near darkness.

The funeral home was a storeroom of the dead more than any single haunted house could claim to be. The number of dead that had made their way through the place doubtlessly had to leave a black mark of some kind. What that mark was, and how deep it ran had only begun to emerge for Norman.

A shadow stirred on the staircase, and their blood pressures shot up violently.

For an instant, the two were frozen in their tracks. They had seen the movement, and were more than ever aware that something was about to happen. Norman tried to urge Phyllis on anyway. He wanted this to be over.

Hesitatingly, he got her over to the stairs and made her go up in front of him. As they inched their way to the second floor, he knew that she would get the full impact of whatever happened. It made him horridly joyous, and in spite of the fear, he loved every minute of it.

The top stair creaked as they passed over it, stretching the tension a little farther as they stared down the hall. The room which had provided the earlier nightmarish experience in Norman's life was at the end of the hall, and too close for his comfort. He had been avoiding it for what seemed like an eternity, but there was a time for everything, and this was the time to scare the hell out of Phyllis.

Suddenly, a darkness appeared at the end of the hall. Its presence was stronger than Norman had ever felt before, and goose bumps erupted immediately from his flesh. It was becoming more and more powerful by the second. How and why didn't matter; only escape mattered. But the presence was all around them, and its crushing weight on their souls made them even more panicked.

With quickness Norman had never seen in Phyllis, she flung his hand off her arm and darted past him to the stairs. The fear holding his body in place was becoming unbearable and movement was totally impossible. The will Phyllis had summoned to break through her fear was far beyond his capacity. He just couldn't move!

Near the top of the stairs, Phyllis's eyes caught hold of a dark figure. It was solid, and

moved steadily toward her, bringing her fear to a
rocketing climax. With the stubbornness and
stupidity that Norman knew were her strong points,
she tried to rush past the figure to make it to the
stairs. The figure lunged out of the way, tripping
her as she tried to push past. Unable to prevent
the fall, she went crashing to the bottom, bouncing
from railing to step and finally laying motionless
a few feet from the stairs.

Sitting in the dark, Harold heard the floor
creaking around him. This place was sure scarier
on the inside than it was outside. His mind was
already playing tricks on him. There couldn't
possibly have been anything out in that hallway
just then. He had just gotten there, and things
weren't supposed to happen until he was ready.

He felt the need to move but held back until
he could see where he was going. The ghosts could
wait for him. They were dead already anyway. As
he looked around, he felt as if someone was looking
right back at him. That was all it took to get him
on his feet.

Making his way to the black hole he figured
was a door, he decided not to use his flashlight.
The ghosts didn't need any more advance notice than
they already had. At least his brain was working
in this old place. His imagination accounted for
the better part of the work, but he could still
manage some simple thoughts.

At the doorway, he thought he heard footsteps
coming from somewhere down the hall to his left.
Listening closely, he was sure of it. He was going
to have to check it out. Either that, or he might
as well turn around and scurry back home to dwell
on his self-defeat.

He had never been a quitter.

With a few quick and quiet steps, he made it
through the door and into the front room. He
couldn't make out any shapes, but he could still
hear the footsteps. Then he shuddered as two loud
simultaneous creaks reverberated through the room.
Checking his automatic urge to flee, he strained to
see what he could, and then stepped further into
the room.

The massive emptiness of the place came to rest on his shoulders, and he ran to the stairs trying to get away from the feeling. His tennis shoes made him more silent than his prey, but he still had a dread feeling that he couldn't understand. It was almost as if he wasn't the predator, but the prey, and he would soon regret his entry into this haunted old place.

The stairs went quickly below his feet and he was soon two from the top. Out of the corner of his eye, he thought he saw another movement. This time, he was sure he had seen it. Cautiously stepping onto the second floor, he began to walk toward the movement, flashlight and cross in hand.

Suddenly, with horrid assurance, a figure came rushing at him. His first instinct was to dive to the side. As he did, his foot caught hold of something solid that almost dragged him with it. Behind him, he heard a series of muffled thuds, but never a scream. That had been a real, live person, and he was in real trouble!

Before he could get up, another figure was rushing at him. Too much in shock to move, he sat and waited for the consequences. A ghost might be better than a real person after what had just happened.

"Phyllis, Phyllis are you all right? Phyllis!" Norman's voice half cracked as he yelled out.

Glancing down, he noticed Harold sitting on the floor shaking and managed to get out "What are you doing here?"

"Don't hurt me." Harold mumbled, trying not to think about what he had done.

"Don't worry, kid. Everything is probably O.K."

Seeing Harold's flashlight, Norman grabbed it up and walked down the stairs to where his wife lay motionless.

"Well I'll be a god damned fool," he blurted out, "her head's twisted clean around!"

And it was. Phyllis was as dead as she would ever be. A thirty-step flight of stairs could do wonders for a body, and it had done so for Phyllis.

The new nursing home director in Breklettin
started his Monday with the project that had been
left him as priority one by the board of directors.
Get all of the deceased patients' papers and
requests sent out immediately. Unlike the last
director, the job meant something to this man. It
meant food for his family, and a roof over his
head. He would work his ass off for this place.
By the end of the day, he wanted to have most of
the papers on their way. It would show the board
that he wanted this job.

At first, the parchment laying spread out on
his new desk went unnoticed by the director. He
had begun to think that he might just need an
assistant to get things rolling a little faster.
As a result of this thinking, he sat down at his
desk to make a phone call. His son would help him.
He was a good kid. They needed to be doing more
things together before the boy thought he was too
old for that kind of thing anyway.

The parchment caught his eye. It lay
plastered to his desk as if it had recently been
wet. The burnt spots dotting it verified this in
his mind, and also brought him the reason it was a
priority job. The paper looked important, too
important to be lying in his office.

Scraping the corner up with his pocketknife,
he felt funny even touching the paper. It felt hot
to the touch, and yet, it had to have been doused
at least two days earlier. The name on the back
sent him to his file for a family record.
Surprisingly, there seemed to be only one relative
of this Eagan Portraire. He had no doubt in his
mind that the relative would be as lost as he was
when trying to decipher the papers. But then, that
would be her problem.

Five minutes later, he decided it would be
stupid to send something that looked so important
by mail. Hand delivery would make up for the time
lost when the former director neglected the paper.
No, that would be a stupid, wasteful use of his
time.

With a quick search through his desk, he came
up with a large manila envelope and an official
nursing home label. Stuffing the pages into the

envelope, a strange thought hit him. What if the paper hadn't been meant for the relative, but another person was expecting to receive it. The thought was so stupid that he shook it off and addressed the package to Janet Portraire anyway.

The day was a pretty good one in Hawthorne, or at least, it was for Marcus. In the past few days, his life had made a pretty good turn around. Besides, his head wasn't throbbing constantly and the seizure auras were keeping their distance.

With all of this in combination, the day went quickly as good ones usually did, and Marcus was home and in a good mood before he knew it. Nikki happened to be in a good mood, too, and Marcus appreciated it more than he would have expected. Something healthy and different would do them both some good this evening, and Marcus knew exactly what it was. They hadn't been on a walk for years, as he remembered it, and this would be a good evening for one. When he mentioned it to Nikki, she got pretty excited by the idea too.

After putting dishes away and changing into shorts, they headed outside for some fresh air.

"I don't think I've even seen this entire little town." Nikki said as they hit the sidewalk.

"Well, it's been awhile since I really had a look at it myself. I don't know where we should head to."

They both felt years younger as the blocks slowly and aimlessly passed. The evening turned to darkness as the Lemontes looked closely at each and every house they passed. The walk was pulling their thoughts together as walks had always done in the past.

As their conversation shifted from one thing to another, it eventually came to the disturbing subject of dreams. Both were obviously uneasy with it, but they fell into the topic anyway.

Pointing to a huge white house as they passed it, Nikki turned to Marcus with a grimace.

"You know, honey," she said, "I've had a dream about that house before."

"What, Nik? Have you ever even seen that place?"

"No, I don't think so. But I know it was in one of my dreams. I remember walking past it, and there was an old man sitting in a rocking chair on that front porch."

As they looked at the bleak old house, Marcus tried to picture what she had just said. Nowhere in his memory could he recall seeing any people out on that porch. And there was a certain weirdness about the house. It had two front doors, and practically no windows. In fact, the front was shovel-faced, if that was a good term for it. It was just a box with a porch.

"Do you remember anything else?"

"No, that's all, just the old man out on that porch. But I'm sure I've never seen the place before now."

"I don't know, honey. You could have driven past here sometime and just happened to have glanced at it."

"I don't think so. Let's get away from here though. It's starting to give me the creeps."

Speeding up a little, they were soon out of sight of the white house. Their pace didn't slow down for several more blocks where they came to a small bridge and stopped for a rest.

"Can I have a kiss?" Marcus asked quietly.

"Of course you can. Do you think you deserve it though?"

Before he could answer, she had locked onto his mouth and didn't let go until a passing car interrupted them. Their love was still alive, and possibly even growing. It was strange how trouble could come and go so quickly in their lives, leaving only its small tracks for them to remember. Maybe all marriages were the same way. But then, it didn't really matter now.

"Are you ready to go on?"

"Only if you are."

But she knew that he wasn't, and she wasn't either. Just holding each other on this little bridge in the darkness was all they wanted right then. The simple things had always been the best for them.

After about twenty minutes, and hyped up more than ever, they continued their walk. They could continue their closeness at home later, and both knew that they'd probably be up pretty late doing just that. The walk would continue to invigorate them, making it even easier to stay awake.

The blocks went by quickly, and they soon found themselves in the worst part of Hawthorne. Even in this small town, a certain fear of bad neighborhoods could creep into people's lives. Evil was universal, and Hawthorne was no exception to the rule.

"I don't like it here." Nikki said, clinging to Marcus's side. "Why don't we turn around and go back?"

"Anything you say, honey. After that white house, I'm not up to being in this area myself."

Instead of going back the same way they had come, they would go over a block so they could see new things. They also, without actually saying so, wanted to avoid the white house on the way back. Something about Nikki's dream was troubling, and they would rather figure it out in the morning, or at least in daylight.

As they approached the block the white house sat on, they turned down another street to avoid even seeing it. There definitely wasn't any reason to tempt fate, especially when it concerned them and a future child. Marcus had learned from his funeral home experience, and Nikki wasn't any stupider.

But as the two got farther away from the place, the effects it had rendered wore off. They were soon talking happily again.

Crossing through the center of town, they occasionally stopped to gaze in a store window. Most of the time, it was too dark inside to see anything. But they didn't care. They weren't really looking for anything anyway.

Quickly bored with the stores and their meaningless contents, Marcus and Nikki moved on and were soon in residential areas again. Being an old town, Hawthorne was filled with huge houses that had been around at least since the turn of the century. Even though Marcus had lived in the town most of his life, some of these old houses seemed as new to him as they did to Nikki. One of these

108

soon came up on the opposite side of the street and
caused him to stop, pulling Nikki back with him and
nearly bringing them both to the ground.

"Wait a minute, Nik. There's something over
there in that yard. Can you tell what it is?"

"Marcus..Don't do that to me. I'm scared
enough, and that house looks creepy anyway."

"No, I'm serious, Nikki. There's something in
that yard, and I don't like the looks of it."

"Well, why don't you go over and look at it.
I'm staying right here though."

Crossing the street, Marcus glanced back at
Nikki. She was huddled up and shaking, even though
it wasn't cold outside. She was as afraid as he
was, only smarter and still on the other side of
the street. Curiosity dictated that he see what
was in that yard.

When he got to the curb at the other side, he
stopped. He was close enough to the house to see
that it could easily have been used in the old
'Addams Family' series. Staring intently into the
darkness at the figure, it slowly cleared in his
vision. It was a statue of a winged dog with
lion's legs and huge fangs. It was a demon statue!
A sudden flood of images from old horror movies
filled his mind and he stumbled back a few steps.
This was just too much for one night! Turning and
running back across the street, he could almost
feel the thing drilling a hole in his back.

"Come on, Nik." He said as he pushed her
ahead of him.

"What was it, Marcus?"

"It was..it was a demon statue, a winged dog
with all the trimmings. And that house....it was
so terrible looking. It almost made our funeral
home look like a toy store."

They were both really scared now. Marcus
became silent, and the silence only made things
worse. They were going home. As fast as they
could, they were going home.

Making there way down a huge hill, Marcus
suddenly stopped cold. Tears came to his eyes as
he stumbled backwards grasping at air that wouldn't
support him. Nikki turned, and her eyes caught the
terror that was in his face.

The dark figure from his dream had been on the corner ahead of them.

"What's wrong, Marcus? What did you see?" Nikki asked frantically.

But Marcus only stood there, his eyes too full of tears to see anything anymore. His legs buckled, and he fell to his knees, a faint smell of hotdogs and popcorn drifting in.

Nikki, heart pounding erratically, knelt down in front of him and looked into his eyes. They were frightened eyes, eyes full of more fear than she had ever imagined possible, especially in her husband.

"Marcus...Marcus, honey. What did you see? You have to tell me. I want to know."

Still unable to speak, Marcus looked down to avoid her eyes. He didn't like for anyone to see him cry, especially not Nikki. There was just no way he could avoid it. He had seen what he had seen, and it would have been enough to send anyone into tears. His dream had come to life, and there was no way he could escape it by waking up. He was already awake...

"Squeeze my arm." He said them being the first words he was able to get out.

"What, Marcus?"

"Squeeze my arm!"

Grabbing his arm, she squeezed. Lightly at first, but he made her squeeze harder and harder until her hand cramped up and she had to let go. What's gotten into him, she thought?

"I am awake." He said as the aura drifted back and faded away again. "This is the worst nightmare I've ever had, and I was awake when I had it…. We have to get away from here, Nikki. We have to get home. I don't feel safe out here anymore."

"O.K., honey, but you have to tell me what happened on the way home. Will you?"

"When we get home, and behind locked doors. Then ...maybe.."

Jumping to his feet, Marcus took off for home, leaving Nikki behind. She had to run to catch up to him, and she practically had to keep running to stay by his side. Occasionally, he glanced back over his shoulder to see if someone was following them. His eyes were still watering, even as they approached their own home twelve blocks from the hill they'd just been on.

Slamming and locking the door behind them, Marcus walked to every window in the house, closed his eyes and shut the drapes. Then, and only then, did he sit down with Nikki, who had followed him to each and every window.

"Nikki, I saw him."

"Saw who, Marcus?"

"The black figure from my dream, I saw him on that corner. He was there one second, and gone the next. I saw him! My dreams are coming to life! What am I going to do?"

"Just calm down, Marcus, you're safe here with me in the house so just calm down."

"But I saw him. I know I did. He was all in black, and he was staring at me. And then he was gone. I know he was there, I know it! Didn't you see anything?"

"No honey, no I didn't. But I know you did. I've never seen anyone's eyes look so afraid. I believe you really saw what you say you did, and it scares me to think that something could scare you so much. It terrifies me!"

No matter how hard he tried, the picture of the figure in his mind plagued him for the rest of the night. Nikki could see this, and tried as hard as she could to distract him, but he would still drift off. He had seen it. They both knew it, and they could only hope that he didn't see it again. That neither one of them saw it for that matter. If they were lucky, it would be a solitary, freak occurrence and whatever it meant would fade from their lives.

Norman struggled through a strange day. Phyllis's untimely demise had thrown him a little, even though at the back of his mind somewhere, he had wanted her dead. She was really gone now. He didn't know whether to party or to mourn. A decision would just have to be made, he thought to himself with a slight chuckle.

The funeral had gone smoothly without him even

shedding a tear. The people in the town must have thought him to be either a stoic old rock or completely devoid of emotion. That was their problem though. Soon, Janet would be over to see the recent widower, happily enabling him to forget his sorrows. She was good at that, as good at it as Phyllis had been at nagging him into the ground. Why had he ever married the witch in the first place? A question he was happy not to have tormenting him any longer.

It was nice how so many people had brought him such good food. Cooking was one thing Phyllis had been good for, and he would have to suffer without now. It was only a small suffering though, and nothing to compare with what he had gone through when she had been alive. He could learn to cook. That, or Janet could come over and cook all of their meals for them together. That was probably the way that things would turn out. Sounded pretty good to him, and she would surely be happy to do it.

The phone rang as Norman got up from the kitchen table to go to the bathroom. Who could that be, he thought. Maybe it was Janet calling to say that she would be over right away to see him. That would seem strange in itself, her being there in the house that Phyllis had so recently lorded over. But as he got to the phone, it stopped ringing. Only three rings, that was peculiar wasn't it? People who called him usually let it ring for hours. That is, if he didn't quite feel like answering it!

Heading on to the bathroom, the phone again started to ring. He rushed to his bedroom and the nearest phone to answer it, but again the phone stopped ringing just as he got to it. Something was definitely going on here. If it happened one more time, he was going to take the phone off the hook for the rest of the night, Janet or no Janet.

A little pissed off, he returned to the bathroom, and decided that while he was there, he might as well take a shower. If the phone rang while he was in there, it would just have to wait. He was getting tired of the pranks.

But the phone didn't ring while he was in the

shower. In fact, it didn't ring until he was again
sitting at the kitchen table. This time, it was
Janet.

"Who have you been talking to?" she asked with
a slight amount of anger evident in her voice.

"I haven't been talking to anyone. Every time
the phone rang, I picked it up and there wasn't
anyone there. No, that's not even the way it's
been. I haven't even gotten as far as picking up
the stupid thing before it stopped ringing."

"You definitely had to be talking to somebody.
I've been calling all evening."

"That's impossible. The phone didn't start
ringing until about an hour ago, and then it only
rang two times."

"Norman, why would I lie about this? There
must be something wrong with your phone then,
because I know what I've been doing all evening."

"Why don't you just come over here, Janet?
We'll talk about this when you get here."

"Oh..all right, Norman. But I don't really
want to talk about this anymore. I'll be over in a
few minutes."

Hanging up the phone, Norman returned to his
place at the table to wait her out. Maybe there
was something wrong with his phone. He couldn't
think of any other reason why she hadn't been able
to get through, unless it was Phyllis's ghost
trying to put a stop to their little affair. That
one would be good for a couple of laughs later.

For twenty minutes, Norman sat at the table
waiting. What was keeping her, he thought? She
was usually quick about doing the things he wanted.
Surely, that wasn't all going to change now. Not
that he was the type of person who would use
anybody or anything like that. In fact, it was
usually the other way around. At least it had been
with Phyllis.

He was starting to worry about her when he
heard her car pull into the driveway. Getting up
to let her in, he glanced out the kitchen window.
For a second, he thought he saw a figure on the
corner at the end of the block. But then it was
gone, and the doorbell was ringing.

"Did you just see someone standing down there

on the corner as you pulled in?" he asked Janet as she came through the door.

"That's a nice way to greet me. I wish you wouldn't try to scare me like that. I've had enough of a scare with that stupid phone of yours."

"I'm sorry, honey. I just thought I saw someone down there, but I guess it could have been my imagination. That phone business kind of got to me a little, too."

"Well, O.K. Give me a hug, and I'll feel a lot better."

Taking her in his arms, he gave her a good hard hug. Before he let go of her, he grabbed her butt, and she let out a fake squeal.

"I'm not ready for that yet, Norman. Give me a chance to calm down a little first."

"But I don't want you calm, honey."

"Well, you certainly don't want me tensed up the way I am right now either. Neither one of us will enjoy it if I am."

"I don't know about that, but I guess whatever makes you happy. What took you so long getting over here anyway?"

"I just took my time. That's all."

"Why? Are you mad at me because you couldn't get through on the phone for so long?"

"Yes, I was getting mad. But I'm not mad anymore. I just didn't feel like rushing myself."

"That's nice to hear. Put Norman on hold for awhile so he can sit here in his kitchen and worry until you get here."

"Don't be crude, Norman. You know I wouldn't do anything for such a stupid reason as that."

"I guess you're right. I'm sorry, honey."

"That's O.K. I guess you have had a pretty tiring day with the funeral and everything. How about we go ahead and hit the sack? I'll make you forget all about that terrible funeral and anything else that's happened to you today that you want to forget."

With no verbal reply needed, they shed their clothes as they walked to the bedroom, and were soon too occupied to see the figure standing at the window.

CHAPTER 8

The store was worse than it had been for months. Matt's employees seemed helpless, or at least, more helpless than usual. He felt like he was a slave to them all. His lunch break was coming up, and he felt like taking off to St. Louis …or maybe China.

At a little after one o'clock he found himself near the front door, and without a word to anyone, he escaped. If he hadn't taken the opportunity, he would have never gotten out. It was great to be free. If he could really take off to China, he'd be gone. He didn't have anyone to go with him, but he could manage all alone if he just took a shot at it. He'd made it this far without a woman at his side. Why not keep it that way for a while. An image of Nikki flashed through his mind, but he slapped it down with a brutal stroke of conscience that surprised him. Maybe there was hope for him. He would have to eliminate all thoughts of her. She was taken, and even more so now that she was pregnant, end of discussion.

Speeding out of the parking lot in his Jaguar, he had a strong urge to take off on a car hunt. But what would his people do without him, he thought sarcastically? He really didn't give a shit after the morning he had just plowed through. After a quick stop for gas, he sped out of town for the second time on such a mission. This time, he would actually make it out of town.

The road was pretty clear since it was mid-afternoon, and Matt made good time to Patton. He was in a good mood now, but he didn't feel like looking in this town. A thought came to him, why not go over to Wellsly and pick up Terry. He could convince him to go along for the ride wherever it took them. His little escapade was turning out to be better than he had expected. To hell with the store, it wasn't going to bind him into slavery today.

An hour later, he pulled into Wellsly, and quickly came across the plant nursery where Terry worked at the edge of town. Matt hopped out of his car and ran in to talk to his old friend. When he found him, a shocked smile gradually took over

Terry's face.

"Matt! What are you doing here?"

Again happy to have such an effect on someone he knew, Matt felt a surge of confidence in his impulsive decision. "Thought you might like to go on a little car hunting expedition with me, Terry, how about it?"

Looking around in clear disbelief, Terry quickly said, "I can't just take off. I don't own the place you know."

Still confident, Matt didn't hesitate "Well, I could use the company, man. Let me make you an offer. If they won't cut you loose for the day, quit. I need a partner in the store, and you're it."

"What! You were serious? You had better think about it again, because I might just take you up on you're offer."

Sure of himself, Matt said, "I've thought about it more than enough. Are you going or not?"

Five minutes later, Matt had a new partner and a wingman on his car hunt. He was definitely going to make this a good day. All he needed now was to find the new car of his dreams. That might be a tough one since he didn't exactly know what the car of his dreams was today. But with a day like this one though, he was bound to get something.

"How did you manage to get away from the store today, Matt?" Terry asked as they hit the highway heading for St. Louis in the much wealthier Sioux Nation, and car lots galore.

"I couldn't deal with the place anymore today, so this is my escape. You'll be my relief, though. With you helping me run the place, I'll have half the work that I do now. I might as well fire the rest of the staff now. I think that we could handle the whole place ourselves."

"Just as long as you don't go back on your offer now, Matt, it's a pretty safe bet that I'll agree with anything you want to do. I still can't believe this. If I had been married or anything like that, I couldn't have done this. But, you know how it is."

"Yup, I'm afraid I do."

"Well, anyway, I hope you have a place for me

116

to stay when I first get there. I also hope that your....our business is doing good right now."

"An easy yes to both questions, you can stay with me for as long as you need to, and the business is well into the black right now as it always is. I've been thinking about getting a roommate for the past week or so anyway after that nightmare. The place is really starting to get to me, living there alone and everything. Well, you know what I'm talking about."

With things pretty well settled in Terry's mind for the time being, the car settled into a comfortable silence. The drive took them rapidly toward the western end of the Shawnee Nation. Things changed dramatically as they emerged from the northern edge of the Shawnee Forest. The trees could apparently lull you into believing the whole Nation was doing as well as Hawthorne. The shocking truth would have been difficult to imagine. The first impossible to ignore change was the fields that were surrounded by twenty foot high, razor wire topped chain link fencing. These appeared at pretty frequent and increasing intervals. They would occasionally catch sight of soldiers patrolling the perimeters of the fenced land, and not just soldiers, but heavily armed Apache soldiers. The soldiers were predominantly guarding fields of livestock, but occasionally they would spot a soldier on the perimeter of a field that was being used to grow crops. There was nothing like this near Hawthorne or within a hundred mile radius of it. On first sight, Terry's initial impression was "HOLY CRAP!" This was followed by a few quieter and less intense "Holy crap"s until all he could do was stare.

"I can't believe this." He eventually said still looking out his side window. Matt decided the statement was directed toward him since he was the only other person in the car.

"I know, I've seen them hundreds of times before. You don't get out of the Forest much do you?"

"I guess not. This stuff would be hard to forget."

"Yeah, and it only gets worse in the flatlands

farther north. Didn't you at least hear about this at the university?"

Glancing toward Matt, but quickly turning back around to stare out his window, Terry said softly, "Well, probably. But it's pretty hard to accept or even consider accepting until you've actually seen it."

"We have it pretty good where we are, or at least where I am and where you're going to be."

Terry settled back into his seat silently and Matt shot some quick looks over at him a few times to see if he was all right. Matt had never seen anybody react so intensely to a bunch of fences. But then they weren't exactly normal, everyday fences. The people who owned that land had a serious interest in protecting it, and he could understand that as a businessman himself. Most of the fenced land was owned by businesses in other Nations, and if they had been burned by theft in the past, they were determined to prevent it from happening again in the future, some a little more ferociously than others apparently.

Following the initial shock caused by the fences, the rundown towns they intermittently passed didn't provoke a response from Terry. Wellsly wasn't exactly a booming metropolis, and he had spent quite a few years since college finding that out. Poverty wasn't new to him. He had grown up as an orphan and only managed to go to college on an urchin grant from some stranger or business in a Nation bordering the Shawnee Nation. The donors were never revealed, but anyone who got a grant knew it was an attempt to make them productive, law-abiding citizens before they abandoned the Shawnee Nation like most eventually would. The chance to go to college had turned him around so the program was apparently working at least somewhat.

The view began to change as they neared St. Louis, Sioux Nation. Gradually, the giant fences tapered off and the towns grew in size and prosperity. The transformations were as unmistakable as the abrupt changes he had seen as they drove out of the Forest. By the time they neared the inter-Nation bridge, there was probably little difference between the Sioux and the Shawnee sides. Clearly, the best area on the Shawnee side surrounded the Eastern Intertribal Council complex at Cahokia, a long abandoned native city. The wealth in this small area easily matched that in any other Nation, but then, the wealth was coming from other Nations along with their tribal representatives. Cahokia had become a virtual utopia in comparison to the rest of the Shawnee Nation.

When they made it al the way into St. Louis, the car hunt turned out as well as Matt could have ever expected. Looking in a large city in a much wealthier Nation greatly increased the selection. After two or three stops, he found the car he couldn't do without.

On the way home in his new car, Matt was in an even better mood than before. Porsche's seemed to have a way of doing that to people, old or new. Terry felt happily secure in their deal, and their conversation carried on non-stop. They were both riding high in the clouds, and it would take some serious trauma to bring them down.

A day later, the effects of seeing the man in black were still savagely eating away at Marcus. It still all seemed so impossible. Sure, some of his dreams had actually happened in the past. But they had happened before he had the dream, not afterwards. And none of them had come close to being this bad. There was something extremely wrong with it all, and he couldn't put a finger on it no matter how hard he tried. The man, or was it just a dark figure...whatever it was it was horrible, and he needed to know what it meant. He felt like he was having a breakdown, and he hoped like hell it was reversible. What was he going to do? Their marriage couldn't stand another knock like his coma. And the figure...it was going to appear again. He could feel it. But why, why was he so sure of it? He had never been as sure of anything since he had met Nikki. He had been sure of her. That was a good thing though. This...this was something else. It could come from anywhere. He had a hard time even walking through his own

119

house at night now without crumbling in fear. And where would it end? Where would the nightmare end?

Immediately after falling asleep, Hedda found herself in the same place she had been for the past five nights. She continued to be boggled by the cumulative nature of the stupid dream. And now she was in it again. The procession slowly came through the cemetery. The huge vapor eyes appeared and began to stare at her. The hooded figures closed in on her, and then her father revealed himself. From that point, the dream had progressed a little further every night. Various people, people she had never seen before, began to be unhooded. But the significance hadn't yet surfaced. There had to be a reason for it. Why else would she have the stupid dream so many times?

This time, from the depths of the darkness, a figure appeared. It was something new, she thought in the dream, as the dream seemed to roll on in front of her eyes. The figure didn't belong there, and yet it did. The feeling was unexplainable. As the dream continued on, in a sudden and less explainable impulse she yelled at the dark figure.

"You, over there in the darkness, make yourself known to me!"

Amazed by the formality of her own atypical speech, she regretted her stupid behavior immediately as she usually did when she behaved like an idiot in a dream. Hedda dove back behind the tree line to wait for her punishment. But like the past few times, the dream wasn't going any further tonight and its vividness began to fade slowly. Fighting it in every way she could, she tried to keep from waking up. The figure had to be significant. She was sure of it. But then the dream was gone, and she found herself half awake lying in bed with Ray. A safe place to be, she thought. Better than the old cemetery in the dream at any rate, and that made waking up a good thing even if she wouldn't be able to get back to sleep for the rest of the night.

With that thought, she forced herself out of bed to go to the bathroom. Her full bladder was probably why she had woken up, she thought walking down the hall toward their guest bathroom. 'Why hadn't she gone into the bathroom next to their bedroom like always?' popped into her head. It hadn't even registered as unusual behavior until she was almost to the second bathroom. She quickly pushed the thought out of her head. She wouldn't be able to sleep now anyway, and maybe not for the rest of the night. Revived would have been a good word for it, wired even better. Not the way she usually felt half way through the night that was for sure.

As she passed the half-open sliding door to the living room, something peculiar caught her eye. Continuing on to the bathroom, she would have to figure it out after she had taken care of the business at hand.

A few minutes later, she was at the door into the living room again and looking in. The strangeness in the room filled her thought immediately. There was movement in there. She could feel it more than she could actually see it, but it was there. The darkness robbed her of most of her sight. It had to be Ray, she thought to herself. Or did she say that out loud? It didn't really matter. There was definitely something moving in the living room.

As her eyes slowly became accustomed to the darkness of the room, the cause of the disturbance became clear. The old wooden rocker was slowly swaying back and forth. Staring even harder, the horror of the moment hit her with the force of a cannon. Ray hadn't followed her out of the room. The chair was empty!

The room became darker and Hedda slid down the doorframe with an ease that would have been unknown to her any other time because of her age.

Down the hall, Ray had reached out for Hedda to find her side of the bed cooling and empty. Thinking she must have gone to the bathroom, he looked in the direction of the connected bathroom for any light that would prove him correct. But the doorway was open and dark. She had gone to the kitchen then, he thought. But that would be unusual for her. She had to be sick or something.

Jumping out of bed, he hit the bedroom light

switch and grabbed his robe at the same time.
Stepping into the hall, he saw her crumpled figure
on the floor near the living room, and his first
thought was to call an ambulance. No, he had to
get her off the floor.

With a quick flick of his wrist, he lit the
whole hall up, and most of the house with it.
Moments later he found that she was breathing but
her pulse was racing. Gently shaking her, he knew
that she had fainted by the way she lay on the
floor. But the look on her face... What would
cause such a strange expression? She looked
scared, but of what? He hadn't heard anything. He
had been sleeping though, and it would have taken
something pretty harsh to pull him out of it. Not
feeling her next to him in bed had been along that
line, but he hadn't even felt her get out of bed.

The closest place to lay her down was the
living room couch, and he made his way to it after
lifting her from the floor. His heart wouldn't
tolerate him doing this too many times. He was out
of breath before he got half way across the room to
the couch.

An odd revelation hit him, and he glanced over
at the now motionless rocking chair. He could feel
that there was something wrong with the room, but
he couldn't see anything unusual. Everything
looked the way it always did. It sure as hell
didn't feel right though.

A shadow caught his eye, and he turned to
stare into the corner where he had seen it. His
mind was giving him fits, he thought, because there
was nothing there. This was all too much. He
couldn't take much more strain.

"Are you O.K., Hedda?" Ray asked as Hedda
finally came to twenty minutes after he had found
her. "You know, you can't do this to me, honey.
You're all that I have, and I don't want to lose
you."

"What happened, Ray?"

"I don't know....I found you on the floor in
the hall, and brought you in here to the couch."

As Hedda's mind tried to pull back what had
happened to her, her eyes darted about the room
looking for something she wasn't sure she would

know if she saw. Something in the room had brought
her to the floor, but what could it have been.
There wasn't anything in the room that could have
fallen on her and knocked her down. Had she
tripped? She couldn't imagine on what, but then,
anything was possible in the dark.

With a blank look, she stared at the rocker,
hadn't there been something sitting there?
No...That was foolish. Nothing was there now, and
nothing ever was in the old antique. They never
used it.

"Do you think you can make it to bed, Hedda?
Or should I call Marcus and have him come over and
check you out?"

"Don't bother him at this hour. I think I can
make it back to bed, but you had better help me
anyway. I feel so tired now."

Helping her to her feet, Ray led her across
the room. When they were almost on top of the
rocking chair, he had to pull her to the side. She
must have still been out of it a little, he
thought, because she almost walked into the stupid
thing. Maybe he had better carry her the rest of
the way.

"What are you doing, Ray?"

"I'm going to carry you the rest of the way
back there, honey. You're so tired; you almost
walked into the rocking chair."

"The what, what are you talking about?"

"You're half asleep, Hedda. Didn't you see
the rocking chair here by the door?"

Turning around to look in disbelief, she saw
it. It wasn't moving now, but it had been.
Darkness again began to take over her vision, and
Ray held her up as she started for the floor. He
hoped Marcus wouldn't mind a call, because he was
about to get one.

But by the time Ray carried Hedda to the
bedroom, his own heart was acting up, and he
collapsed on the bed. Grabbing for his pills, he
popped one into his mouth and lay there hoping to
feel better, if even slightly. Whatever was wrong
with Hedda was about to push him over the edge. He
had to settle down. She wouldn't make it a week if
she woke up and found him dead beside her.

The pill took hold though, and he was up a short while later to put her the rest of the way into bed. In his pain, he had more or less dumped her half on and half off the bed. She still hadn't woken up... Something was seriously wrong with her. She didn't feel warm, but you couldn't always tell by that.

Maybe he could wait until morning. She was right about waking Marcus up. He wouldn't mind coming over, no doubt, but sleep was precious to a doctor. Morning would show if she was any better. It was probably just exhaustion anyway. She hadn't slept well lately, or at least, this week she hadn't. That was surely taking its toll on her, and tonight showed it.

It was strange how she had been having the same nightmare every night this week, too. She had never experienced anything like this, or at least she hadn't told him if she had. He would have to ask her about it in the morning. But for now, the light in the living room had to be put out, and then it was bedtime.

Turning around, he walked into the hall and headed for the living room. Just before he reached it, he stooped down to check the carpet for any loose ends. He knew there weren't any, but something had caused her to fall and he needed to take care of it.

At the doorway into the living room, he found the carpet was firmly seated as it seemed to be everywhere else. He reached for the light switch, giving up for the night. The sudden darkness sent a chill up his spine, and he found himself rushing down the hall for some reason. It was just a strange and stupid feeling, but he felt someone was watching him.

Quickly closing the door to his bedroom, Ray leaned against it for a while to catch his breath. His heart was again wildly arrhythmic. It was over for him, he was sure of it this time. The dark form in the bedroom corner was the final play of the game. Grasping his chest, Ray fell to the floor, and his body quivered as death took hold.

The final thought to flow through the agonizing pain wrenching his body brought a flow of tears to his eyes. I love you Hedda...good-bye.

Marcus finally managed to pull his spirits up
after several days. He didn't consciously do it;
he just more or less blocked the events of that
previous evening out of his mind. Time had a way
of making horrible things seem not quite as bad for
him. It was a gift that he had developed sometime
in his past, but when, he obviously had forgotten.
Things went well at the office for him, or at
least, better than they had all week. This good
day inspired him to take a drive by the corner
where he had seen the figure. He had to face what
he had seen for a change, and it would be easier on
a good day. The sun was even shining brightly for
him. Maybe, just maybe, it had been a real person
on the corner that night. Maybe some trace of him
was still there. It was doubtful, but there was
always a chance.
Nikki might even want to go with him. She
would if she knew it would make him feel better.
She had really changed in the past few weeks;
especially since she had found out she was
pregnant. The old jealousy bullshit had gone down
the drain now. If he would quit seeing things and
having the damn seizures, his life would really be
pretty normal. There always seemed to be something
going wrong though. With his luck, he probably was
having a breakdown. That and death were about the
two worst things that could happen to a guy.
"Nikki," Marcus said as she answered the
phone, "how about going on a little drive with me?"
"Sure, honey. Where are we going?"
"Uh..I thought we'd go over by that corner.
You know the one that I saw the figure on."
"How could I forget? Are you sure you want to
do this, Marcus?"
"Well, it's a good sunny day, and monsters
usually only come out at night....Yes, of course
I'm sure. Do you want to go?"
"Of course I'll go with you! You're not going
over there alone. That's for sure."
"Good. I'll be over to pick you up in a few
minutes. Bye, honey."
"Bye." Nikki said as she hung up the phone.

She hoped she wouldn't regret this. If it returned him to what he had been like for the past few days, she knew she would. The thought made her sick to her stomach.

But as it turned out, they found nothing. There were no tracks, and there wasn't a way that a person could have come and gone to create such an illusion. What happened had been a case of the supernatural, or more likely than that, purely a mental aberration brought on by his head trauma.

The idea of a breakdown flew back into Marcus's head with the ferocity of a demon. He knew for sure that he was falling apart now. He would rather be dead than lose his sanity and everything that it entailed, Nikki included. He had to take control and that was all there was to it.

Hopefully, Nikki didn't think that he was losing his mind. No matter how much she loved him, he knew that it wouldn't hold up through a breakdown. Hard times weren't far behind them, and he knew that they could crop up again at any time. He had to figure this thing out before it meant the end of his marriage.

The drive home was a quiet one. Marcus was afraid to ask Nikki what she thought of him, and Nikki was afraid that anything she said would show her lack of faith. They were both confused, and to say the least, scared.

Nikki hadn't lost faith in Marcus. She was becoming afraid of him in many ways, but she had in no way lost faith in him. The reasons for her fear were as deep rooted to her as Marcus's reasons were to him. She was sure that he wouldn't understand them either. She sure didn't know what was getting to him. They were going to have to sit down for another talk before it got any worse. Tonight..

The office had become peaceful for Norman since Phyllis's death. No more nagging phone calls, no more hiding his affair, and most importantly, no more going home to the hag. Norman's brutal life had turned to sugar. It made him wonder what would go wrong next.

"What do you want to do tonight, Janet?"

Norman asked as she came into his office for the thousandth time that day.

His admiration for her had increased even beyond what it had been. They obviously belonged together, or at least he felt so.

"Well, why don't we just stay in again?"

"Are you sure, Janet? You aren't getting tired of that are you?"

"No..it's only been a short time since your wife died, and I don't want any suspicion to fall on our affair. I know it doesn't really matter anymore, but I would feel better about it anyway."

"O.K., that's fine with me." He said with a smile.

She was thoughtful. Thinking of their reputations all along was just a small part of it. She was a real wonder to him, and it seemed she always would be.

Time passed quickly for them, but they closed the office early anyway. They were both ready to hit the bed, and they knew each other well enough that evasiveness was well out of their systems. It was becoming impossible for either of them to keep their minds on work. If it weren't for the other realtors under Norman's hire, they wouldn't spend a minute a week in the office.

But as the door closed behind them, the few thoughts they kept for the office passed from their heads. Only pleasure was on their minds now, and they would soon be absorbed in it. If this was love, they had fallen as far as anyone could imagine, and possibly deeper.

The ride to Janet's apartment wasn't quick enough for the two. Their desire was building beyond control. But as soon as Janet had her key in the door, the phone rang. Ringing more than twenty times, she hesitantly picked it up.

As Norman sat down on the couch, he heard Janet hurriedly hang up the phone. A few seconds later, she entered the living room with a blank look on her face that could only mean trouble for Norman.

"Who was that, sweetie?"

"It...It was nobody.. There wasn't anyone on the line when I picked up the phone."

"Then what's the matter, hon? You don't have to take it so hard. It happens all the time."

"I know that. But something was different this time. I didn't hear anything, but then I did.."

"Well then, what did you hear?"

"I don't know. But I heard something, and I don't know if it was words or what it was. It was strange. It was very strange."

"Well, can you put it out of your mind? If not, I think that we might as well go grab something to eat."

"Let's go eat then. I'm sorry, Norman. I shouldn't let this bother me, but it is."

"It's O.K. We have the rest of our lives to have sex, maybe even later tonight, if you're up to it."

"We'll have to see. It was just so strange, and I don't have to deal with this sort of thing very often."

A little depressed by the situation, Norman slowly got up from his seat and walked to the door. His thoughts traveled to later that night, and he hoped that she would feel better. Just having her with him made his life so much better. He would have to keep himself cheerful, and maybe she would feel better.

As they were about to close the door, the phone started to ring again. Looking into Janet's eyes, he saw exactly what he had to get rid of, her uneasiness. Making his way across the room to the phone, his composure was destroyed when the phone stopped ringing as he picked it up.

"God damnit!" He screamed into the phone.

"Come on, Norman, let's get out of here. After we eat, we'll go to your place instead. I think I'll feel better there."

"O.K." Norman said with rage still oozing from his voice.

"That sounds good. We'll take the phone off the hook, too, believe me!"

This time, they made it out the door, and were soon eating shrimp and French fries at Weatherby's. As the evening wore on, they gulped down a large number of drinks, and with them came forgetfulness.

Again, they were becoming aroused. As it built in their bodies, they began to caress each other under the table. Drunkenness gave them the freedom they sought, and darkness provided them with an easy way into the men's restroom. They had never done anything as wild as making love in a restaurant bathroom, but they were soon taking care of that.

The sense of excitement flared even greater as they feared someone might intrude. Sweat began to flow, and as they both lost sight of their surroundings, Janet uttered words Norman had never heard. They seemed so raw and sexual that his whole body tingled.

As quickly as it had begun, it was over. They both felt the wear on their bodies, but they were still too excited to be tired. Quickly exiting the restroom and then the restaurant, they made their way back to Norman's house. Here, they found what Norman had been waiting for seemingly for an eternity, the bed, and its promises of further bliss.

Sobered by their experience, and yet drunk enough to enjoy a brief rest, the phone jarred them from their peace. The two calls at Janet's apartment were long forgotten to them, and Norman picked up the phone wondering who the hell would be calling.

The line was dead. Not just a dial tone, but totally, soundlessly dead.

As he slammed the phone down, the memory slipped back into his mind, and he frowned in disbelief. This couldn't be happening here, too. Who would want to ruin their evening besides a dead woman? Her days of that were well over.

The phone came off the hook. They weren't going to be disturbed anymore tonight.

For some reason, Pete dreaded getting up for the day's paper route. The bed felt really good to him, and the route was getting so boring. Maybe he would change the delivery order again today. He had already done that three times in the past two weeks, and it hadn't helped. He would do anything to beat the boredom though.

Finally crawling out of bed a few minutes

before he was supposed to be at the paper office, Pete rushed out the door without a word to his mom. He was getting to the age where he felt it didn't matter if she knew where he was every minute. She knew anyway, but not telling her every day made him feel independent.

A half hour later, he came to the first house on his route. The supplements he was also hauling weren't that important to people, he thought, so he was going to take his time today. No one would know the difference. Most people threw them away or put them at the bottom of birdcages.

Deciding to zigzag around his route, hoping not to miss anyone, Pete headed for the Lemonte house. Maybe Marcus would ask him in like he had last week. That had been the only good point in his day, especially since he had gotten his hat back.

But when Pete knocked on the Lemonte's door, there was no answer. He knew they had to be up because Dr. Lemonte's office opened in half an hour or so, and he would be going there soon. As he continued to knock, he had an idea. Maybe they were in the kitchen and couldn't hear him. He would have to go knock on the back door, just in case. He really did feel like talking to Marcus today. He had been thinking a lot about the old funeral home, and he needed to ask him a question or two about it.

Leaving his bike behind, Pete ran around to the back of the house, looking in all the windows as he went. At the back steps, he felt someone watching him, and knew that they had to be there in the kitchen. After a few knocks and no answer, he gave up and started back to the front of the house.

A harsh and sudden realization made him turn and look at the funeral home. There, on the grown up front lawn was his father! Turning away, he knew that it was impossible. His father had been dead for over two years!

Another look and his father had gotten closer to him. He was at the edge of the Lemonte's yard, and his hand was raised beckoning him to come closer.

It was impossible! It was just impossible!

He had seen his father in the coffin, eyes closed, and as dead as he had ever seen anyone! This was impossible!

Pete closed his eyes. But fear made them open again, and the five seconds brought the figure to within twenty feet of him. Panic rose into his throat, and he felt the need to throw up. Something smelled horrible, and it was getting worse by the second.

From the front of the house, Pete heard a car pull into the drive. Glancing back to the figure, a dark suited man had taken his father's place. An instant later, it was gone as Marcus Lemonte pulled up beside the wide-eyed, sick-faced boy.

"What's the matter, Peter? You look like you've seen a ghost." Marcus said, regretting it as the boy's face grew whiter and he started to shake after the remark.

Before Marcus was halfway out of his car, Pete was wrapped around him crying so hard it shook Marcus's body.

"Are you O.K., son?"

But it was obvious he wasn't, and he kicked himself mentally for his second stupid question. The boy had seen something, and it had come from the funeral home.

Pete continued to cry, and with a little effort, Marcus picked him up and carried him into the house. When he tried to put him down, he found it impossible. The boy was clamped to him like a vise. The strength a frightened little kid could have was incredible.

About an hour later, Marcus had called in to his office to tell them that he wouldn't be in until eleven o'clock. Pete was calmed down almost to the point of talking, and Nikki had come and gone. Hedda was taking Ray's death terribly, and Nikki had been trying to console her since five-thirty that morning. She somehow felt Ray's death was her fault, and kept mumbling something about a rocking chair.

It was a strange and stressful morning. Ray's death alone had been enough, but to come home from there to find Peter about to have a cow in the side yard....it was just too much. The past few weeks

131

had been like some demented soap opera, and he was getting pretty tired of it. Something was going to give sooner or later, and he still wasn't so sure that it wouldn't be him.

"Pete, can you tell me what you saw out there?"

A few mumbled words came out, and then Pete's voice picked up.

"I saw my father..."

"What, Pete? I thought your father was dead. Didn't he die about two years ago in a car wreck?"

"Yes......I saw my father."

"Yes, your father's dead, or yes, you saw him?" Marcus queried, feeling confused, and hoping the first was true.

"Yes, I saw him, and yes, he's dead!" Pete blurted out before bursting back into tears.

"But that's impossible, Pete. We both know that, don't we?"

Still crying, the boy nodded his head in agreement. Marcus's heart jumped as he thought of something that scared even him.

"Did you see anything else, Pete, besides your father?" He asked, feeling a chill rush down his back.

"No......yeah, I did...there was a man in a black suit.."

As Marcus's eyes began to water, he walked away to the sink to hide his face from the boy. This couldn't be happening to him. He wasn't cracking up, but he knew it would probably be better for him if he were. He wasn't the only one seeing the figure. It was tearing up this little kid's life now, too!

"I think you'd better stay here for the rest of the day, Pete." Marcus said as he finally turned away from the sink.

"No...I can't. I have to finish my paper route."

"I'll take care of that for you. What's the paper office phone number?"

"I don't know. I never have to call in there."

"Well then, come with me, and we'll stop by there. I guess I need to go to my office for a while. You can go with me, O.K."

A spark of light came to Pete's eyes. He had never been as afraid as he was now. Not even the night at the funeral home. But Marcus was making him feel a little better. He seemed to know exactly what he was feeling. Maybe he had been afraid one time when he was a kid, and now he understood. Anyway, he felt safe with Marcus. The thing had disappeared when Marcus pulled up, and now he felt safe.

From outside, a loud noise drew both of their attentions. It was several seconds before they realized it was only a car, and a minute later before their hearts calmed down. Nikki was home.

"We had better hurry up and get to the office." Marcus said to Pete.

But what he really meant was they had better get away before Nikki saw Pete. She had made it quite obvious that she didn't like the boy. And he could see no reason to push the matter, especially with both of them close to hysteria. Nikki couldn't even begin to understand them.

Rushing for the front door, Marcus remembered his car was parked at the side of the house. She knew he was still here, unless she figured he had walked to the office. They would have to now. The kid couldn't be alone, if he had any understanding of what he had been through. They were just going to have to walk.

The sight of Marcus's car in the drive sent a sigh of relief through Nikki's body. All the grief that Hedda was feeling made Nikki realize how much Marcus meant to her. She was so lucky to have him, even though she didn't seem capable of showing it to him sometimes. Maybe there was something wrong with her that she couldn't see in herself. Marcus had to really love her if that was the case. It almost made her cry to think that she had stuck it out with him several times for less than romantic reasons.

Glancing up to the second story window of their bedroom, Nikki saw the curtains close back as if someone had been watching her pull up. Marcus was home, all right. A flash of thought spurred the deep-rooted feelings of love in her, and she rushed into the house in anticipation of seeing him.

As the back door closed behind her, Marcus and Pete were half way down the block toward his office. Nikki quickly climbed the stairs and started down the hall toward the bedroom. There was a slight chill in the house, but she was too excited at the thought of seeing Marcus to notice it. Cold weather was well past by May in Hawthorne anyway.

The sunlit hall began to dim slowly as if darkened by a passing cloud, but Nikki could only think of Marcus. Nearing the bedroom doorway, she could see no signs of his presence, but she knew he was there. He had to be there. She had just seen him in the window. In fact, she had seen his face. He had seemed so handsome in that instant, and even more so than usual.

"Marcus. Marcus, where are you, honey? Don't hide from me."

But there wasn't any response to her words. The room seemed empty as if he hadn't been there at all. He had to be in the bathroom then, and just couldn't hear her.

When she crossed the room, the darkness that had swallowed up the hall began to surround her. Only seeing the brightness of the bedroom window, she didn't realize what was overtaking her. Reaching the bathroom, she didn't understand why Marcus hadn't acknowledged her.

"Marcus! Don't do this to me. Please come out, wherever you are."

Only silence greeted her as she looked into the mirror and saw the hazy darkness in the bedroom behind her. Her thoughts flew through all the possible causes for it, and settled on 'fire'! Panic rose in her throat. She had to get out of the house!

Running into the bedroom, she couldn't smell smoke. What the hell was going on here!

The air began to close in on her, taking her breath away. Total darkness soon surrounded her with a viciousness she had never realized it could hold. And then Marcus's experience in the funeral home floated into her mind. Passing out would be a blessed relief.

As if the darkness could sense her thoughts, the haze lightened enough for her to take a rasping breath. She again started for the hall, but didn't really know if that was where she was heading. She felt herself flounder around the room for what seemed an eternity, barely conscious. The door was here somewhere. Why couldn't she find it? What was happening to her?

Arrangements for Ray's funeral had to be made, Hedda thought as she lay in bed feeling sick at the very thought of it. She knew she wouldn't be able to take care of it. There was no way. She couldn't even look at his closet without breaking into tears. One of their kids would have to do everything for her. They'd be there within a few hours, and they would be the ones taking care of the funeral.

Again, tears took hold of her as she shook in violent spasms that drained her of what strength she had left. Why couldn't it have happened to her? Of course, they'd expected him to die within a few years, but doctors weren't always right. They weren't gods. How could they predict his death, and then just sit back and wait for it to happen while she struggled with every emotion available to her to forget it had even been said. It wasn't fair! They'd had so many problems, and things were just looking up for them. The doctors could all go to hell for what they'd done to her life. They could all go to hell!

Sleep came to Hedda fitfully, but as a blessed escape. In her sleep, Ray still lived. In her sleep, things were as they always had been.

Then, the dream of the past week began to unfold in front of her. The graveyard, the hooded figures, the huge eyes floating in the mist, everything was the same. The figures approached her, and began to reveal themselves. The familiarity of the dream was comforting in its own way. Even when her father revealed his face, she felt no fear. All was good, but doubtlessly not intended to be. Ray's face suddenly appeared as one of the cloaked figures defrocked, and her heart

135

stopped. This was new. He wasn't supposed to be in this now sacred dream.

Looking frantically around, the black figure she had only seen briefly before came from behind the eyed mist. The figure moved towards her, closer and closer, until it was within inches of her face. Her stomach churned as it had never done before in this place.

Abruptly, the figure veered to her left, and journeyed again into the mist. Relief swept over her, and she again began to view the unmasking of the other figures. Comfort returned, and fear no longer held her tensely in its grasp.

With her attention taken totally by the unmasking of the figures, she failed to notice the eyes. The bulbous objects were slowly beginning to swirl as the mist had done earlier. The eyes moved in and out in patterns that she didn't notice. The eyes reached a certain point, and kept to it lessening their swirls, but increasing their speed. Darkness began to grow from within this point, a deep darkness that eventually caught Hedda's attention.

Nothing escaped the darkness that was forming. Even the eyes which seemed to be forming it were eventually trapped, and disappeared forever into the void.

Hedda tried to develop an answer, but there was no explanation for the nothingness. It only grew, taking everything with it. The figures began to be swept up in the blackness, and were disappearing as the eyes had done. She watched as her father and then Ray were carried away into the growing blackness.

When all were gone, the blackness no longer spread. Again, relief seemed to fill her body. It was almost over. She could feel herself beginning to wake up. The dream would soon be over, and for once, she welcomed it. Too much was happening and it wasn't right this time. It couldn't be the same dream, and yet she knew it was.

Watching the blackness, an even greater darkness began to form within it. It would have seemed impossible an instant earlier, but it was happening. The darkness took form, and the dark

figure soon emerged from it. And then, just as
Hedda's eyes popped open from the dream, a gently
swaying rocking chair appeared beside the figure.

What had been nothing in her mind the night
before now became all too clear to her; evilness
beyond her comprehension was going to kill her. It
was going to take her life, and any that might be
tied to her. The evil was upon them.

A harsh realization struck Nikki as she groped
for the door of her bedroom. She wasn't ever going
to see Marcus again. She wasn't ever going to have
their baby. Tears came to her eyes, and she fell
to the floor giving up to what seemed a lost cause.

From out of the darkness that surrounded
Nikki, a figure emerged. Still near the point of
passing out, she couldn't make out the person who
was there. She only hoped that they would hurry
and save her. Although she didn't know what was
happening to her, she did know she wanted out. Out
of this room, and out of this house for good.

The figure neared her, and when it was a step
away, Nikki reached for it. She missed. But that
was impossible, she thought. It was right there
nearly on top of her. Didn't it see her? If it
was Marcus, why didn't he see her!

Curling herself into a ball to prepare for the
force of a body falling on top of her, she waited.
The shock never came. Had she imagined the figure?
Maybe she had even imagined seeing Marcus in the
window.

A strange feeling overtook her. She felt
weightless in the haze of the room. As the feeling
became stronger, she felt the softness of a bed
come between her and the floating sensation. She
had been moved from the floor. By what, she didn't
want to know. But she had been taken from the
floor and moved to the bed by someone or something
that she couldn't see or feel!

Fear clawed at her heart as she prayed for
Marcus to find her. She needed him now more than
ever. Even the love he felt for her wouldn't bring
her back if this person killed her. He had to help
her! Now!

A weight came down on her, the weight of a

body. NO, she thought. Not to me. Not with a child resting in my womb. Marcus's child and the child of the only man I could ever really love. This can't be happening to me!

She began to cry as the weight on top of her forced her legs apart. She would rather die than have this happen. "I love you, Marcus!" she screamed. "I love you, Marcus! Please help me! Please forgive me for this! I love you! I love you, Marcus!"

The weight came down harder, and she could feel her pants being torn from her body.

"Marcus... "

As a door slammed downstairs, the haze cleared instantly. A second later, Marcus's face was staring in horror at the half naked body of his wife stretched out on their bed. Anger overtook him immediately, and then she turned her head towards him. The look on her face… The tears streaming from her eyes… He saw the misery in her eyes and rushed to her.

"Marcus.." She cried. "It was awful...it tried to rape me, but I couldn't see who it was!"

As Marcus fell to the bed beside her, tears came to his eyes and the grief of a thousand deaths poured into his stomach. He couldn't do anything to protect her. She had almost been raped, maybe even had been, and he couldn't do anything but hold her now... Laying there in the once safe and comfortable security of their own bed, the two cried. They cried until they couldn't cry anymore, and then they held each other for the rest of the day, forgetting food and everything else that would have made the day normal. Their lives and their marriage had been violated in a way that could never be forgotten. Marcus wanted to kill the man who had done this to her, but it would be impossible to find him without the slightest fraction of a description.

Thoughts poured through their heads. Reasons evaded them, but the thoughts came to them freely anyway. Thoughts of the funeral home and the problems it had already caused in their lives, thoughts of the man in black, thoughts of death. Would there be no end to the ruin of their lives?

Eventually having taken as much comforting from Marcus as she could deal with, Nikki got up from the bed and made her way down to the kitchen. Marcus had to be hungry, even though she knew she wouldn't be able to bring herself to eat. She had to take care of him, otherwise, he might not understand. Losing him would send her over the edge.

A few minutes later, Marcus came down to check on her. "Honey, I'm not really hungry. Don't go to any trouble for me, O.K."

"But I want to, Marcus."

"You don't have to though. You know that, don't you?"

"Yes...no, I don't know.. I did, but not anymore.." And tears again came to her eyes as the pain and confusion swept over her.

"Oh, honey. I love you so much. I love you, and nothing can change that."

"Are you sure? Nothing...not even this?"

"Nothing."

They had spoken enough. There was a little comfort in just being together, but the cut had been a deep one. In the back of Marcus's mind, he wanted to know exactly what had happened. But he knew now wasn't the time to work it out. She needed time to straighten things out in her own mind first. So much had been going on lately. It was amazing that they had held up this long. He couldn't think about the rest of it now. She needed all of his attention.

Darkness overtook the house rapidly, and neither one of them had realized it until it was almost ten o'clock. They were in their own world, a world of self-pity and remorse. Time meant nothing to them, and they felt nothing to go along with it.

At eleven-thirty, Marcus picked Nikki up and started to carry her upstairs. She didn't resist him as she usually did when he wanted to carry her. She needed him close to her and would allow anything to keep him there.

When he had gotten her up to the bedroom, he put her down on their bed and she curled up into a ball immediately.

"Honey, I'm going downstairs to shut the lights off. I'll be back in a second."

"Marcus, don't go. Just leave the lights on for tonight. Don't leave me alone up here..."

"It'll just take a second, honey. Then I'll be right back. I promise"

"Please don't leave me!"

He went anyway. He didn't want to hurt her, but she would have to get used to being in the room again.

Practically taking the steps in a single jump, Marcus quickly made it to the kitchen. The lights went out, and total darkness engulfed him.

Upstairs, the haze began to surround Nikki's body as she lay there watching it overtake her. She tried to scream, but the words failed to escape her mouth. The haze had her, and the weight again fell down on her body.

Approaching the stairs, Marcus's imagination began to take him away. An old fear swept over him as he mounted the stairs. What if someone reached through the rails at his side and grabbed his feet. The horrible implications of this threw him into flight, and he skipped as many steps as he could fearing the hand that would grasp his ankle.

The impossibility of what was happening to her for the second time that day dawned on Nikki. At the same time, she realized she had fallen asleep for a brief moment, and this nightmare had been just that.

Marcus came walking quickly into the room. She was glad to see him, and realized that his hard breathing had been the sound that woke her.

"What's the matter, honey? Did you run up the stairs or something?" Nikki asked, feeling the drowsiness of her dream slip away.

"Uh..sure, Nik. Just trying to get back up to you so you wouldn't be afraid, is that O.K.?"

"Why of course it is, honey. I'm glad that you got back so fast. Now climb into bed so that I can hold you."

Feeling he had managed to get away with being scared without Nikki knowing it, Marcus got into bed beside her and gave her a suspiciously large kiss. She knew. He could tell by the twinkle in her eyes as he pulled away from her lips.

CHAPTER 9

The days went quickly for Matt and Terry after they joined forces at the clothing store. Matt felt like the weight of a million worlds had been lifted from his shoulders. Not only that, but he now had a friend who was less than a phone call away. That alone tempered some of the fears that were building from the nightmares he was still having. The nightmares were worse, but he could cope with them now that Terry smoothed out the rough edges at the store. The coming night held promise for further proof of that. They had been invited to, of all things, a costume party. Spending their lives surrounded by clothes, often weirder than the costumes they made, was obviously not enough for two girls at the store. Attending the party was a major shift in Matt's usual store policies. Before this, he and his employees had lived in different worlds even in a town the size of Hawthorne, the immigrant pride of the Shawnee Nation. It wasn't what his father would have wanted, but he was dead now and the decisions were Matt's to make. It had worked well until now. From the moment Terry heard about the party, his mind had whizzed to the possibility of making some new friends and maybe finding a new girlfriend. His life had improved tremendously and a girlfriend seemed to be the next step. He actually had a future now, and could imagine having someone to share it. Matt wouldn't be much help on his quest, having the same problem himself. But Matt had grown up here and couldn't see beyond his history with the people of Hawthorne. There was such a thing as knowing too much about people after all. But this wasn't the case for Terry. It was all new to him and he planned to seize the brief opportunity before the store ruined it for him.

As the day rolled around to evening, Matt was also beginning to think along the lines of a future spouse as a result of Terry's excitement. All of his years had failed to provide him with even one steady woman in his life. It was unlikely that this night would be any different. This same desperation in college was what had driven him to desire Nikki. But she had been happy with Marcus, despite some rough times. She was taken and he had never accepted it. His best bet would be to find someone to take his mind off her. Terry believed the party might just provide that. Determination was all that he needed, that and a hell of a lot of luck.

"Well, Terry. What do you think of this get up?" Matt asked as he made his way out of the bathroom.

"Almost as good as mine." Terry said laughing.

They had both chosen the late fifties, early sixties, hippie look complete with shoulder length wigs and peace medallions.

"We had better get out of here before I chicken out on this nonsense." Matt said as he took another quick look in the mirror.

The ride to the party was a silent one as they both tried to psyche themselves up. By the time the sounds of the party met their ears, a determined look had found its way into their eyes.

"Ready to make a fool of yourself?" Terry asked as they stepped from the car and headed for the source of the loud music. It was a wonder the cops weren't already there to harass the partiers. At least that was the thought that lingered in Terry's mind until he stepped through the front door. Standing there like bodyguards was what appeared to be the town's entire police force.

"Uh..hi boys." Terry said as he quickly stepped by them "Having a good time, I hope."

"No problems here." One of the officers said as he lifted his half-empty beer cup up to the two men. "Just making sure things don't get out of hand."

Cops! Small towns were truly amazing. The mayor was probably floating around the place somewhere in a drunken stupor.

Look over there." Matt said, trying to get away from the cops like he had just punched one in the mouth. "Isn't that Sue?"

"What" was all Terry got out before he was shoved half way across the room by Matt's hurried movements.

Hitting a small clearing in the middle of the living room, Matt stopped a minute to catch his breath. While standing there, Sue actually did walk up to them and start a conversation. Since Terry had only met her a few days earlier, he more or less stayed out of the little chat that went on between the other two, and drifted off to find his own company. The resolve was still raging in his blood, but if he started to think about it too much, he knew it wouldn't last.

"What do you think of the party so far?" Sue asked Matt as she hung close to him so he could hear her.

"I don't really know. We just got here a few minutes ago."

"Well, I've been around the whole place, and you're the best thing that I've seen so far." She said pulling closer to him.

It was obvious she had been there quite a while. She was already drunk enough to make a pass at him, and he was her boss.

"Uhh..why don't we get to someplace that's a little more quiet." He quickly suggested.

Threading their way through the crowd of people, Matt's naive view of the girl's simple drunken pass at him didn't register. Inexperience was a big problem in his love life, and wasn't about to be fixed without a few letdowns.

After about twenty minutes, they finally made it to the back door and freedom. The talk began and continued for several hours with Matt feeding Sue a steady flow of alcohol. Gathering his courage, he managed to ask her to go back to his house with him for a few more drinks.

"No..," she mumbled, "I've had enough to drink. But if you want to go to bed, I'm game."

The shock of her words hit him instantly. This was incredible. She had actually asked him to go to bed without any of the crap that he had expected he would have to go through. More than likely, he wouldn't have either. He would have

143

ended up driving her home after hours of hinting conversation on his part, and been severely depressed afterwards. This was great! Without a further thought, Matt hurried Sue to his car, totally forgetting Terry. There was only one thought on his mind. A thought that constantly plagued him but was always unfulfilled. Sex!

He made the drive back to his house in record time. His anticipation far outweighed his worry of a ticket. Besides, most of the police force was drunk back at the party. Even the one cop who had caused him so much trouble since he had returned to Hawthorne was there, drinking like everyone else. The bastard was a two-face, and that was the one thing that made Matt madder than anything in the world. To think that he had been pulled over for a DUI by a cop who, in uniform, was now drinking like a fish at a large, out-of- hand party.

The front door opened easily as always, and he helped Sue through and to the bedroom. Hospitality was out. He was too ready for this, and she was too drunk to care anyway.

As he undressed her, he could feel himself needing her more with each passing second. He tried to hurry, but only fumbled with her buttons, and had to slow down to get the job done. He had time anyway. The house was his, and Terry wouldn't disturb him even if it wasn't.

Finished, his clothes came off easily, and he slipped into bed with her, excited beyond anything he had ever felt. Ecstasy was at hand, and he would enjoy every bit of it.

Taking control, he began a routine that, although unpracticed, seemed to come to him as naturally as drinking beer. Lust was all it took to drive the sexuality out of him, deeply rooted and unused as it was.

Slowly driving her to her first climax, Matt felt the joy that most of the world, with the exception of him, had managed to feel in their lives. As she squirmed around and occasionally let out a slight gasp, his own need began to overtake him. He was going to have to get inside her.

As always, he fumbled when it was really important. This time, however, as he slowly began to lose his patience and the desire to enter her faded, Sue acted, even in her drunken state, to pull him out of it. It was as if she knew he was having trouble. In fact, she did know. Experience, drunk or not, kept them going. But the time quickly came and went, and they were both soon about to fall asleep. Matt hadn't been able to control himself, but Sue was too tired to mind.

A loud crash at four AM brought Matt jarringly awake. Before he could even struggle into his pants, he heard pounding throughout the house, and fear swallowed up his sanity. The thing from his nightmares was coming to get him, and he had nowhere to go! He was going to die!

It was now just outside his door. He could feel its presence, and he was going to have to deal with it. Maybe death wouldn't be so bad. In a way, he had always enjoyed peacefulness, and death would be no more than that. Permanently!

The door suddenly slammed open, and the total terror that had built in Matt's soul sent him back against the wall and crashing into his nightstand. Lying against the wall, Matt stared in horror at the figure standing before him. At first, recognition failed him, but then there was only disbelief. Terry, a ragged and bloody mess, fell to the floor at the foot of his bed.

A scream issued forth from the other person in the room, and Matt realized that Sue had woken to see the same hideous thing he had.

"Shut up! Shut up you stupid bitch!" flew from Matt's mouth before he could control it. There would be no further relations between them. Partly because of what they had both just seen, but mostly because of his stupid words. It didn't matter to him now anyway. His best friend lay on the floor half dead, and all the stupid girl could do was scream.

Getting to Terry as fast as he could, Matt saw the destruction to his friend's body. Without turning him over, Matt could see that Terry's left arm was almost twisted clear of his body. His clothing was soaked through with fresh blood draining down his face from the large flap of skin and hair partially attached to his skull. It had to have happened just a few minutes before he made it to the house.

Frantically, he got to a phone and called for an ambulance. He knew it would take at least twenty minutes for it to get from Patton to the house, but he didn't dare do anything else. He tried to stop what bleeding he could without disturbing Terry too much, but he knew the internal damage had to be unbelievable. He was struggling to breath and his pulse quickly became weaker slowing the flow of blood. Terry had been to hell and back and would only make it if he had an unequaled lust for life.

As Sue sat on the bed in a state of shock, Matt ran back and forth from the bathroom bringing towel after towel to mop up the slowing blood flow. If his will alone could keep Terry alive, he would make it through this nightmare. He knew there was a lot more to it than that, and feelings of hopelessness began to overwhelm him.

Terry's eyes opened, and Matt listened as he struggled to get out a few words. Almost inaudibly, he managed to choke out what he could.

"You left me...I..I was walking home.." But he passed out again, and this time, Matt thought it was for good.

The ambulance arrived, and the paramedics tried everything they knew to save Terry. Barely keeping him alive, the ambulance screamed off to the hospital. Matt wanted to go, but they wouldn't let him with the situation as desperate as it was. He would have to follow and give information to the desk when he got there. They had to be sure the bills would be paid before they'd save his friend's life.

Soon after, the minutes crept by in the waiting area outside of the emergency room and Matt began to wonder if they had taken Terry to another hospital. There didn't seem to be anyone in the damn place. He had always hated hospitals. They seemed to be about the most inconsiderate places on the face of the planet. Snooty doctors and bitchy nurses were the problem. They lived in their own little world, and just couldn't stoop down to anyone who wasn't in the medical field. Patton

146

sure had one hell of a hospital for its massive
population of fourteen thousand. High quality
doctors probably flocked to the place. That is, if
high quality doctors were inept enough to be in the
lower twenty percent of their class.

Just as he was about to start tearing the
place up for answers, a short, pudgy nurse came up
behind him.

"Are you here for Terry?" she asked as if she
was about to get off work and this was her last
duty.

`Yes..yes, I am. How is he? He isn't dead,
is he?" Matt asked, trying to hold back the anger
festering in him due to the hospital's lack of
consideration. "What took so long anyway?"

"Just take it easy there, we've been working
on him from the moment he arrived, and we didn't
think it would be appropriate to tell you anything
until we were sure of his situation."

"Thanks a hell of a lot! Sure, I don't need
to know. It would only make me worry more, my ass!
What's wrong with you people? Do you think you're
gods or something?"

"Listen sir, I'm not going to tell you
anything until you calm down enough to be able to
handle it. Now, are you going to calm down, or am
I going to have to leave you alone until you do?"

The anger flashed in Matt's eyes, but he
fought to control it. It was important to know
what was happening with Terry, and if the little
bitch wanted him to be calm, he'd show her just how
calm he could be. Cold, of course, but calm all
the same.

"O.K., I'm all right. Now, tell me what's
going on with my friend."

"You can't see him now, for one thing." The
nurse said as she looked into Matt's cold, almost
demonic eyes. "He's in critical condition, and
he's been rushed into surgery."

As the nurse began to walk away, Matt grabbed
her shoulder and whipped her fat body back around
so fast that her head spun for a few minutes
afterwards.

"Is that all you're going to tell me?" Matt
asked coldly, keeping a firm grip on her shoulder.

Cowering below him, the nurse felt her body shrink as the illusion of his increasing size hit her like a thousand pound weight. He was going to kill her, she could feel it. Words began to flow from her mouth like water, and she slowly lost control of her legs until she dazedly walked off.

Matt casually walked to the first chair in sight and sat down. The nurse's mouth was getting on his nerves. He had heard enough.

"I want to know where you were tonight, Janet!" Norman yelled as she ran into the bathroom of his house. "God damnit! If you're going to live here with me, I think I have the right to know what you do at night!"

"It's none of your business! I just went out, and you're going to have to live with that, or forget about having me here."

There was nothing Norman could do. He had let her go out on Friday night without him because she had asked for a little time alone. Everything would have been fine if she had come home at a decent hour. But she hadn't. She had found her way back to his bed at about three o'clock, and had enough alcohol on her breath to knock him over.

Then there was the change of clothes she had made sometime in the night. He remembered exactly what she had been wearing when she left, and it wasn't what she had on when she got home.

The idea that she had been with another man hounded Norman to the point that he could almost kill her. He knew she had been. He could smell it on her. It was a strange smell, too. She had probably picked up the first scummy bastard she had found, and taken him who knows where, maybe to the office.

As the thoughts continued to pour through Norman's head, Janet sat in the bathroom looking at her legs. The torment that Norman seemed to be going through meant nothing. The streaks of blood on her legs made her wish he could be right about her. The thing was, she didn't remember, and couldn't tell him anything because of it. Even if she did know, it wouldn't be something he would want to know. The blood must have been the cause

of her change of clothes. She just didn't
remember.

Drifting through her memories of the night,
the last thing Janet could recall was being at some
party. But where the party could have been, and
who threw it escaped her as easily as what happened
afterwards, it was all a blank. Even the clothes
she now had on were unfamiliar, and definitely not
her own.

Whether Janet remembered or not, Norman knew
in his mind what had happened. She had seemed so
perfect for him. He had made a mistake though.
This little affair of theirs was over.

As soon as he got home, Pete locked himself in
his bedroom and cut the old baseball cap that his
father had given him into tiny little pieces. The
event that day had him shaking so bad he could
barely hold the scissors.

After sitting there for what seemed an
eternity, he felt he had to talk to someone.
Making his way through the house, his mother was
nowhere to be found. She had gone to the store.
It was shopping day, and she had gone to the store
for the week's groceries.

He had to find someone else to talk to.
Harold came to his mind. He hated Harold's guts,
but Harold had been with him when he had seen the
ghosts at the funeral home. Maybe he could help
him with what had just happened. Marcus had made
him feel a little better, but he was an adult, and
adults sometimes pretended to understand so that
you'd feel better. Besides, he had turned around
and gone back home before they even got to his
office and sent him home alone for some reason,
adults were really weird sometimes.

It took a lot of courage for Pete to call
Harold. More than he would have been able to
gather had it been for any other reason. This was
important though, and without hesitation, he dialed
Harold's number.

"Is Harold there?" He asked when a woman's
voice answered at the other end.

"Well, I don't know. Hold on for a second."
The wait was a short one, and Harold's

screechy voice was soon bursting from the phone.

"Yeah, who is it?"

"It's Pete, Harold. I need to talk to you really bad."

The sound of disbelief came into Harold's voice. "Pete who?"

"Pete Blair. Can I talk to you, or what?"

"Sure, go ahead. Why are you calling ME to talk, though?"

"We can't talk on the phone. I don't feel right about it. Can you come over here?"

"Well, I guess I can, when?"

"Right now!"

"O.K." And Harold hung the phone back on the wall. This was pretty weird. Blair had always hated him. Why did he need to talk to him so bad now? It would be worth the ride over there just to find out.

About an hour later, Harold was knocking on Pete's door. Pete rushed him into the house like the plague was outside waiting to get in, and pushed him all of the way to his bedroom.

"I hope you have a good reason for calling me over here, Blair." Harold said in the usual jerky way that he talked to Pete.

"I want you to tell me everything that you know about ghosts." Pete said flatly.

"What!"

"You heard me. I want you to tell me everything that you know about ghosts and monsters and everything else like that."

Harold's edgy voice cooled off a little as he felt proud because he had knowledge that someone else actually needed.

"What do you want to know about those things?" He asked eagerly.

"Everything, I want to know everything."

"Can't you ask me some specific questions? I can't just sit here and tell you everything I know."

"O.K. then, you know that night at the funeral home? Did you see those things through the window, or was it just me?"

"I saw them."

"Well, what were they?"

"I guess they were ghosts. Isn't that what you think?"

"Yeah, but I wasn't sure. I hadn't ever seen a real ghost until then. Then, and today."

"What? Where did you see one this time?"

The time went quickly as Pete told Harold what had happened to him that day. From their place in the bedroom, they heard Pete's mom come by with her groceries, and that was all that they heard besides each other's voices. They talked for at least two and a half hours before they ran out of things to say.

"I don't know, Pete." Harold said now, feeling friendly towards his once bitter enemy. "I really would like to go over there again and see if something else happens."

"Why? You still don't believe that I saw that thing today?"

"No, I believe you. I just want to see it for myself."

"I don't know if I ever want to go over there again. Besides, my mom won't let me out this late at night."

"You can spend the night with me. My mom won't even know that we're gone."

"I don't know, Harold..."

"Come on. It'll be fun."

"Well, O.K., I'll ask my mom."

Not really wanting to go, Pete's luck was shot down when his mother said he could go to Harold's. There wasn't any way for him to get out of it either. Harold was standing right beside him when he asked. He had to go...

Too soon afterwards, Pete glared at Harold in disgust as they trudged toward the funeral home.

"This is really stupid, Harold. I can't believe we're doing this."

"Don't worry about it, Pete. We'll be O.K."

"And how can you be so sure?"

"Because I've been in there before, and nothing happened to me."

"What! You didn't tell me that! When were you in here?"

"Remember when that real estate man's wife fell down the stairs in here? I was in here that

151

night. I saw the whole thing."

"Then why wasn't your name in the paper? If you were a witness to what happened, why didn't they question you?"

"Because they didn't know I was in there. The man whose wife died told me to just get out and not say a word to anyone."

"Oh..Harold, you're lying to me. I know that couldn't happen. Those things only happen in the movies."

"I must be a movie star then, because it happened. I'll show you where it all happened as soon as we get inside here. You'll see. There's even blood on the floor, if they didn't clean it up at least."

By this time, the boys were in through the window Harold had used on his first night there. The foul smell of the place hit Pete's nose with the force of a cannon. If it didn't smell better in the other rooms, he would throw up. He always did when he smelled something as bad as this.

"Let's get out of this room." He whispered to Harold, trying to hold his breath at the same time.

Harold made no objections. The smell was getting to him, too. They got out into the hall, and carried the smell with them. It soon dissipated with the drafty air making their noses and stomachs feel better. With the nausea gone and nothing else to avert their attention, fear of the unknown took hold. A shadow and a movement on another wall were all it took to send their heads darting back and forth at the slightest sound.

At the foot of the tremendous staircase, Harold used his flashlight to look for the blood he knew had to be there. It was there, too, a huge dried spot of it. They could even see where one of her arms had been by the print it had left in her blood.

"I think I believe you now." Pete said timidly. Even so, his voice echoed throughout the entire funeral home. Both boys cowered into the shadow of the corner. Whatever might be in the funeral home now knew they were there, too.

"Well, Pete, let's go ahead upstairs. I'll show you how the lady tripped."

152

"How do you know she tripped, Harold? Don't tell me she fell over you, because I won't believe you."

"Whatever you say."

A smile came to his face, and Pete knew that this was as true as Harold being there that night in the first place. Harold had killed the lady by being here that night. A morbid thought hit him, but he shrugged it off. At least, he tried to shrug it off.

Climbing the stairs, Pete kept a close eye on Harold. He was a tricky one, it seemed. He might even like killing people now that he had a taste for it.

With Harold to worry about, Pete forgot the real reason they had come to the funeral home. The thing he had seen that day pretending to be his father was no comparison to a twelve-year-old killer who just happened to be standing right beside him.

The sudden darkening of the staircase behind the boys escaped their attention. Pete's, because he was worrying about Harold, and Harold's, because he honestly just didn't want to believe it was there. For a few minutes, the darkness hovered at the base of the stairs. In that time, the boys managed to get to the top and start down the hall.

The darkness moved in on them. They didn't know it was upon them until a force came down on Harold's shoulder, sending him flailing to the floor. His collarbone had been broken instantly, and had shattered into his lungs. The gasp Pete heard brought him abruptly around. Spurts of blood came from Harold's mouth as he tried desperately to yell out a warning.

The blood was all that was necessary to send Pete running down the long hall away from the stairs. Terror leapt at his heals, driving him faster that he had ever run in his life. It never dawned on him that he had been in this hallway before. A time when he had woken to find he was only in a frightening dream. He wasn't quite so lucky this time.

The hall never seemed to end. Reaching for a doorknob, the walls shrunk away from his hand. He

153

knew what infinity had to be now. Infinity was
this hallway.

Suddenly, hands emerged from the walls and
clawed at his body. He couldn't escape them! They
dug into his skin bringing blood with every slash.
The depths of darkness at the far end of the hall
began to swirl swiftly. He had to get to it. An
irrepressible force had been placed inside of him,
and he WOULD reach the end of the hall. Still, the
clawing of the bodiless hands tore him to shreds,
and the pain was agonizing. He had to keep
going...he had to..

An image emerged from the dark swirls. He
wanted to be there. His father needed him. He
could see it in his sad eyes. He would get to his
father, and everything would be fine. It had to
be... His father would only be there to help as he
always had been, until he died. The thought of him
being dead didn't register. He was in pain beyond
anything he would normally have been able to
handle. But this wasn't normal. He was a young
boy who was seeing his father, a father who had
been dead for two years, and had left an unfillable
gap in his child's life. A gap that needed so
desperately to be filled, that Pete would take his
father in any way that he could have him.

A hard crash on the right side of Pete's head
sent him tumbling. He fell and fell until only
darkness kept him company. And then there was
nothing.

Janet sat at home crying the entire next day.
She hadn't even seen the package arrive earlier
that morning. When she did see it, the package
from the nursing home scared the hell out of her.
Someone had found out about the blood-covered night
she had experienced without knowing it, and now
wanted her to pay for a funeral. No, that was
insane. Her nightmare had just begun last night.
A lot more time and trouble would pass before any
such bill came into her possession. She had to
settle down and think sensibly before she could
open it.

The letter opener rested in her hand now as
she started to open the package. It seemed to her

the opener could be used for a much better purpose right now, but suicide had never been something she was capable of. She had always believed that things just couldn't get that bad. With a shaking hand, she slit the package open and the contents dropped onto her lap. The burn marks and water stains that covered it tricked her eyes into believing nothing else was there on the pages. The small, practically illegible print held its place on the pages, however, as she soon realized. The words, if you could call them that, meant nothing to her. Not only that, but there was nothing else in the envelope to explain what it all meant.

It had to be a hoax, a sick joke that some idiot had thought up to scare her. Maybe Norman had even done it to get back at her. The fire that had been steadily burning in her hearth to warm the chills sweeping over her body caught her eye. The best thing for this package was the fire's burning hunger for fuel.

One page at a time, the three pages of the manuscript went into the fire. Watching with joy at the victory she had just accomplished over some heartless asshole, the pages began to fill with more words. Not scribbles like the others, but totally legible ones. The heat brought them out, not even singeing most of the remaining paper.

Stupidly, she reached for one of the pages causing the skin on her hand to scorch and instantly break out in a cascade of blisters. She had a page though, and the others came out more easily with the poker that stood by the fireplace.

In an effort beyond her usual capacity, she ignored the pain of her burning hand, and plopped to the floor to read what had apparently been translated on the pages.

The previously invisible wording on the pages flowed into her thoughts. To the best of her understanding, her uncle had translated it. He believed he had stirred up a lot of trouble in this sleepy little town, and seemed to be regretting it for some reason. As she read, the insane story filled her head with nightmarish visions. The old coot thought he had opened up the spirit world, and now expected her to deal with his ridiculous problem. The guy had really lost it! What a load of shit!

The whole thing brought the first smile of the day to her face. She knew of Eagan Portraire, of course. Everyone did. The stories of his escapades had plagued her since coming to Hawthorne. He had been the first member of her family to make it to the Nations. She hadn't even realized he knew of her presence until the package arrived. He had always been locked away somewhere because he was a world class lunatic.

As she picked the package up again and started to throw it in the fire, another piece of paper fell to the floor. The paper must have been stuck to the plastic lining, she thought. Grabbing it up from the floor, she realized that it was actually an old photograph. Slowly turning it over in her hand, a sudden chill raced down her spine. A man stood in front of an old funeral home, the one on Restview Way, but obviously in its better days. The picture was black and white and very dark, but the haze around the man was unmistakable. It was impossible, but there was no doubt in her mind. There was something surrounding her uncle. This was the dark figure he had written of! She was relatively new to the Nations and couldn't accept some of their beliefs, but her uncle had apparently swallowed it all, hook, line and sinker.

CHAPTER 10

The hospital found Matt easily because he had been making trouble for them since he arrived. He hadn't left the hospital, and still sat in the same chair that he took after his spat with the nurse the night before.

The surgeon sent a nurse to give him the news that Terry died during surgery in spite of all their efforts. The damage was too severe and as Matt had imagined, the internal damage had been extensive. He had continued to bleed internally while he was here, and all of their surgery had done him no good. Recalling his thoughts, Matt asked "What kind of internal damage? Was it in his head? That's where the blood was pouring from."

The nurse hesitated, unsure how much she should divulge to the man in front of her.

"I'm sorry, sir. I don't think it's my place to give you anymore information."

"WHAT!" Matt's voice rose as the intense anger returned. "I've been waiting here, he's my friend, and I want to know what the hell happened!"

The nurse began to shake with anxiety. This was definitely not in her job description. Now angry that the surgeon sent her to do his dirty work, she decided to get the screaming monster off her back. She had nothing to gain or protect in this and the patient was dead. She would take the man to his friend.

"Come with me." she said, still upset and shaking. She didn't deserve this, so she would push it off on someone else.

Matt stormed after her down the hall and deeper into the hospital with the anger that raged inside him only covering up the hurt that he felt, he had just lost his best friend... When he walked into the room behind the nurse, the sight of Terry's lifeless body brought the full impact of the situation back to him. He had started to believe that maybe this was all a dream he had festering in his mind. Not the kind of dream that he usually had, but something in him was changing and had been for the past few weeks. His attitudes were changing. This incident with Terry was driving him up a wall. Only a few weeks earlier, he might have passed it off as nothing, well probably not, this wasn't nothing…

Staring at his recently alive and vibrant friend, he couldn't utter a word, not even in anger. This was unbelievable, just fucking unbelievable. He couldn't accept it. He reached out and touched Terry's arm, an arm that was already getting cold. This was real and not part of a new nightmare, not a nightmare of his sleep anyway, but a nightmare all the same. He suddenly felt lightheaded and started to drop out, but the nurse watched his face turn ashen and managed to push him back into a stray chair along the wall.

157

She held him upright in the chair as his vision went black, and then he slowly slumped against her. He stayed that way for several minutes, and then began to revive, feeling like he had been attacked and nearly killed himself. The scene and the situation didn't register at first, but his horrid reality slowly returned and he could do nothing more than lean heavily against the nurse. Terry was still dead on the gurney in front of him.

Restlessly, Matt tried to get up and leave the room. He couldn't take this anymore. But his legs wouldn't hold him and he slumped back into the chair. His friend should have made it. He was alive, breathing and alive. The nausea pushed him back into his anger. The hospital would here about this. They hadn't done everything to save him! They had fucked up somehow and they would pay for it!

"I want to see the chief surgeon!" Matt screamed when he finally recovered enough to stand up.

"You have to be quieter, sir." The nurse said. "We have a lot of other patients here who can't afford to be disturbed."

"I don't give a damn about any other person in this hospital, and you had damn well better get the chief surgeon down here for me!"

"That could be awhile, sir. He's probably in surgery right now."

Her words were gradually beginning to shake again as they came from her mouth. This man was enraged enough to kill someone in order to get to the chief surgeon. He would have to settle down a little again before she sent him to the doctor.

But Matt couldn't let the rage inside of him burn out. He didn't know why, but a certain amount of guilt for Terry's death kept creeping up on him, and he had to subdue it in whatever way he could.

The sudden sense that he had killed Terry sent him flying through the hospital in search of the operating rooms. He had to take this out on someone else. He knew he hadn't even been near Terry that night. He had been in bed with some girl. The idea that it had been his first girl had lost its novelty to him. Now, he couldn't even

158

remember her name.

The doors rushed in and out of his sight until he came to the operating room corridor. The chief of surgery had to be in one of these rooms, or so the nurse had said. Maybe she had tricked him though. Menials in fear of losing their jobs often lied to protect their superiors. If she had, she would pay for it!

All of the operating rooms were shut down. The whole corridor lay dark and quiet. She had pulled one over on him. In his rage at realizing this, he punched one of the swinging doors within his reach causing it to fly inward and break several glass objects in its way. A different nurse passing the front of the corridor started to run for her station upon seeing this, stirring up his rage even more. He dove at her, pulling her to the ground.

"Where is the chief of surgery?" He screamed into her face.

"I...I don't know..." She squealed out as she began to cry.

"Goddamnit!! Where is he!! Tell me before I break your fucking neck!!"

Totally breaking down, the nurse could do nothing but cry. Losing even more control in his rage, Matt lifted his fist to punch the nurse's whimpering little face. A force from behind him held his arm back, and then he felt two or three men yanking him back against the wall.

"Someone call a guard!" Came from one of the men's mouth and sent Matt into a flailing fury to get away from them.

A punch to his stomach did nothing more than rile him as he swung out in all directions, landing his fists on every part of his holders bodies. Their grasp on him loosened, and he felt freedom.

He had lost his need to see the surgeon. Now all that he could think about was getting the hell out of there. He had to find someone to comfort his misery. He had to get out of this hospital!

The moment Matt got to his car, he knew where he had to go. Even if Marcus were home, Nikki would surely listen to him. He needed her help now. He didn't need her, he just needed her help.

As a matter of fact, he had no desire for her at all anymore. This realization had just come, and now he knew that all he wanted was her sympathy.

With the roar of his engine, Matt felt his car take to the road. In his rearview mirrors, the hospital people who had chased him all of the way to his car slowed to a stop and gave up their chase. He had escaped. Now only twenty minutes separated him from Nikki, ten as fast as the new Porsche was flying. This time...this time would be the last that he saw her. He had to move on.

A disturbing thought broke through his adrenaline.

He would be alone in his house again now.

As morning came, Harold's parents frantically called in search of their boy and his friend. They didn't usually worry about the things he did, but a dread feeling ate at their guts. He wouldn't be home this time. Something had happened to him. Something far beyond what they had always expected for him. Their dreams had told them so.

By noon, Pete's mother was at their house along with three hung over policemen. None of them had any idea where the boys could have gone.

With the day dragging past, the parent's called every one of the boy's friends, but the results were always negative. Eric hadn't even known where the boys were, and all three parents knew he was both of the boys' best friend.

The possibility of them being runaways eventually occurred to one of the cops. Kids ran off a lot in the Shawnee Nation. It was a tough world out there, and two twelve-year-old boys wouldn't make it more than a few days, especially with no money in their pockets. That had been checked. The little amount of money the parents knew the boys had was still where they always kept it.

"I never should have let Peter come over here last night..." His mother kept saying. Her bitter face hardened and lined by the exhausting work that had kept her and her son in clothing and food for the past two years, plagued the other people in the room. They all wished she would go home and vent her despair on someone else, or shut up at least. Finally, one of the policemen offered her a ride back to her own house, fearing that she was in no condition to drive herself. The atmosphere lightened with her departure, but only until their thoughts again turned to the boys.

By eight-thirty that night, the Shawnee Nation Investigative Unit had been called in to investigate the disappearance of Pete and his friend Harold. Panic had left the parent's that morning, and regret filled its place as the day went on. They relived the problems they had caused for the children, and the problems the children had caused for them. Thoughts of how they had gone wrong in their upbringing plagued them. Had it really been so bad for them that they would run away? The SNIU seemed to think it was the most likely reason for their disappearance. The agents confirmed the local police claim that kids in the Nation ran off pretty frequently. It was a well-known fact in other parts of the Shawnee Nation where hoards of people took off seeking a better life.

All of the people who had been in contact with the boys within the last two weeks were called to the police station for questioning. If the boys had been acting strange, the SNIU wanted to know. If they had been hanging around with 'the wrong crowd', they wanted to know. The SNIU wanted to know anything and everything. What they wanted, however, made no difference to people who couldn't answer the questions. Everything had appeared normal to the people involved with the boys, all of the people except Eric.

From the first call he had received that day, Eric had been mystified by the fact that Pete and Harold would even speak to each other, let alone run away together. Something had happened to them that night at the funeral home, and it had changed both of them. Pete hadn't even called him since that night, and Harold was acting weird, too. When he talked to him, all he wanted to talk about was ghosts and monsters and things that made Eric lose sleep at night.

When the police station called Eric in the

next night, he debated on whether to tell them about the funeral home. Kids weren't supposed to hang around there, and the SNIU might put him in jail for being at the place that night. When they found the two boys, they might put them in jail, too. It all made Eric's stomach turn.

But the SNIU men were nice and offered him a soda when he got there. It wasn't as bad as he had expected. They assumed Pete and Harold had just run off into the Forest somewhere and had gotten lost trying to get back when they finally picked up enough sense to return. Eric knew kids didn't just run off in Hawthorne, but the men made it sound so real that he eventually believed it could happen.

The funeral home came up briefly, and he was relieved when it was quickly passed over with a "We'll check it out."

Eric returned home feeling secure in the SNIUs 'lost in the Forest story'. The dark figure standing on the corner as he rode his bike home caught his attention. The figure had been showing up in his dreams lately, and probably had leapt from his imagination on account of his friends being missing.

When the figure appeared on the next corner, Eric glanced back down the street believing that his mind was playing tricks on him. The dark figure was still there, too! Eric couldn't see into its eyes. In fact, the figure seemed not to have a face at all.

The need to move faster pushed Eric past the figure in front of him. If he hadn't lived on that block, he had a feeling he would have seen it again. In fact, he knew that he would have seen it again! It happened that way every time in his dreams and now it was coming true!

As Eric jumped from his bike and ran for the front door, his eyes darted from side to side in fear of what would come next. The front door held fast. His parents had gone somewhere and locked him out! Tears came to his eyes. He had nowhere to go...

Leaning his back against the door, he waited for the inevitable approach of the figure. He would be brave and face it. He didn't want to die like he came so close to doing in his dreams. But it would happen. The dream was a prophecy, and he had read a lot about prophecies at the school library. You can't escape fate, and the prophecy of his dream had determined this as his fate.

The seconds slowly passed by, however, and nothing happened. When his parents pulled into the driveway, the sound sent him running toward their car. He felt safe now. His parents would protect him from the figure.

With Ray's funeral in the past, Marcus and Nikki made their way home. It had been a long day for them and going to bed was all they could think of. They were beginning to see that hitting the sack at seven-thirty didn't always mean people had boring lives.

"I think Hedda's taking this pretty well now. Don't you?" Nikki asked as the lock clicked on the back door.

They now kept the house tightly locked after her attempted rape several days before. Nikki wanted the place locked up as much as Marcus did, and that made him feel better about her whole story. If he had walked in on her and Matt that day, somebody would have died. The odds were that it wouldn't have been him either.

The house felt calm as the two walked through to the stairs. Although there had been a hell of a lot of trauma in both of their lives in the recent past, at least they were both still alive. Nothing could be as bad as one of them dying, and it made them appreciate each other that much more with each passing day.

With the bedroom steps away, Marcus felt the tension build in Nikki's body. He knew that their stay in this bedroom would never quite be the same. It was a good thing there were three other bedrooms in the house. A move to one of these would have to be made.

In an effort to make the night better for her, Marcus pulled Nikki back from the room and towards the bedroom down the hall. A strange look came into her eyes, but faded slowly as understanding took its place. The change would be good. It would be stupid to put it off. Marcus's old bedroom, whatever memories it held for him, no longer held peace for them.

He had never stayed in any of the other rooms before, but that didn't matter. Maybe it would be better for them both. Even though the rest of the bedrooms held a certain mystique, and had since his childhood, they had held his parents and grandparents, not a bunch of monsters.

With those thoughts in his mind, Marcus took Nikki into the room his grandparents had once occupied. The smallest room on the second floor, it had a certain coziness to it that no other room in the house could match. A feeling of safety emanated from its antique contents. The night would be spent here.

They both fell into bed, absorbing the comfort it held. Sleepiness quickly overtook them, eliminating the usual need to take their clothes off. What the night could possibly hold for them never entered their minds. Only sleep in its never-ending desire for control of life now consumed them.

Trauma shook the Lemonte's night three hours after they had been in bed. The house had slowly been chilling for the past hour, and the cold restless sleep brought a dream to Marcus's fleeting peace.

From the coolness of his place in bed, Marcus got up to find another blanket for Nikki and himself. The realization that the air was not just cold, but frozen, struck him as odd. It would take more than one blanket to fight this off! It would take a whole pile!

The linen closet with all of its enclosed warmth could only be reached by leaving Nikki. Moving through the room in the darkness, he had to make it to the first floor. The closet was nestled beneath the staircase, and he dreaded every step of the journey.

The cold hallway floor hurt his feet, but he had to suffer a little to make Nikki comfortable. It had always been the way of their relationship, and this moment was no different than the past.

A movement from behind frightened him slightly

for some reason he couldn't comprehend, but the
fear didn't last. Only warmth held importance
right now. Even the thought of Nikki didn't bring
him pleasant feelings.

At the base of the stairs, the need to go
outside took him to the front door. There had to
be snow on the ground for it to be this cold.
Early May had never been like this. 'An ice age
coming' floated to his mind. No, something else,
but what could it be?

Nothing...

And then, the funeral home called him.

Yes, the funeral home called him! He heard
it! He felt the vibrations of the sounds as they
screamed through the air and plunged into his ears.
The time had come to face the rapist, and the power
of the mysterious offender would not stop him.

The walk across the yard to the funeral home
drenched his feet. The grass didn't feel cold at
all. The house had been colder, and being away
from it felt really good. Something about the way
the place kept calling him made his skin crawl, but
he couldn't think about that now. Skin can't crawl
anyway, he thought. If he remembered right, he had
read a medical journal on the subject one time, and
the whole idea had been totally blown out of the
water. Skin just didn't crawl.

The calls became stronger as he walked faster
to get into the warmth of the funeral home. It
would be really warm in there like it always had
been in his younger years. His bed on the upper
floor waited for him to return as it always did.
And then, when he got into it, it would absorb him
in its warmth. Just as the funeral home itself
would do.

The front door of the funeral home opened
easily to let him in. A brief feeling of
wakefulness rattled the dream making it feel real.
But he knew that he still lay in bed with his wife.
He could hear her deep intakes of air. His legs
felt extremely tired though, and he did feel cold.
Again, sleep held him in its grasp. But the
realness of the dream scared him.

The slight fear that began to build carried
over into the dream as he entered the funeral home.

The place seemed to glow with warmth. It felt just as he expected. Now he only had to get to his bed upstairs.

In an instant, he made it to the top of the stairs, and began the well-remembered walk to the room with his bed. Soon, his life would be totally pleasant, he would be lying in his funeral home bedroom, and be amidst all of its isolated safety.

A sudden shift in the dream brought him to the top of the funeral home's basement stairs. He had never been allowed to go down them, and what he might find here sent a rush of excitement through him. Now he knew why he had been summoned. The ultimate wish of his childhood stood before him. He only had to walk down these stairs to break a lifelong fear his father had instilled in him.

Again, the dream undertook a radical change. He now stood as a little boy at the top of the same stairs. He stared up into the eyes of his father who kept mumbling words that he couldn't quite understand. Occasionally, the word 'monsters' floated down from the huge mouth of his father, and he shivered at its mention. He had heard a lot of stories about this old place in his short life, and hearing more, from his father no less, scared the hell out of him. Adult thoughts crept back to him, and he found himself at the bottom of the stairs.

A door stood halfway open. He knew what it had to be, so he stepped quickly toward it. A slight breeze came through pushing his hair back from his face. The door flew open the rest of the way exposing an office room with an oak desk the length of a church pew. The desk faced out from a wall of bricks that looked recently erected.

Seating himself at the desk, he began to look through the drawers as if to find what had been so long forbidden him. Something here had great importance, and he now knew that a ghost hadn't been the real cause of his denied entrance.

He didn't find anything in the drawers, however, and his eyes lifted to the other articles in the room to look for clues. From the far reaches of his mind, he realized there was movement behind him. It crept up from the depths and began to cascade around him. Ghostly figures flowed from

the wall behind him and surrounded him, blocking
his view of the door. He panicked as the room
filled with their hazy malicious presence. He
could feel the hatred flowing from the entities as
an unbearable din of voices filled the room. The
temperature in the room plummeted, and he could
feel himself blacking out from the pain he felt in
his ears.

The coldness of the downstairs abruptly woke
Marcus. He now found himself perched in the old
easy chair in his living room. As the sleepiness
wore from his mind, he stared out the window
towards the funeral home. The dream had seemed so
real to him. There could be no possible way that
it had happened though. The smell of hotdogs and
popcorn faded into obscurity.

Then it struck him that he no longer lay in
bed with Nikki. How had he managed to get
downstairs and into this chair? The idea that he
might actually have gone to the funeral home in his
sleep rocked his brain. And then the figure
appeared in his view outside the window. It stood
there, making no movements, but terrifying the
living hell out of him.

Jumping up to shut the curtain, he glanced to
his right. The figure stood outside the front
window, too! Terror attacked his body, and panic
followed sending him to every window to pull the
drapes. At the kitchen window...at the bathroom
window..the figure was staring at him through every
one! He had to get upstairs! The thing couldn't
be there...

Racing up the endlessly long stairway, the
idea of being grabbed through the rails forced him
against the wall. He didn't have time to fight off
anything that might go for him. He had to get to
Nikki!

Entering his own bedroom, he rushed to their
bed to save her from what had now moved in on their
lives. She was gone! He had lost her already!

A slight gasp echoed through the hall, and he
knew he had made a mistake. They had been in
another bedroom that night.

Another gasp filled his ears, and he feared
what he might see when he finally got to her. He

had been tricked. The thing had sent him into his wild nightmare just to get at Nikki.

More gasps came, and words followed, words that brought tears to his eyes. Running frantically to the other bedroom, his eyes caught hold of a sight that would burn into his mind forever.

Nikki laid spread out on the bed. Her body pushed up into the invisible rapist as he was surely lunging into hers. The words floated from her mouth defiling everything that they had ever meant to each other.

"I love you, Marcus...I love you. Don't stop now, please don't stop."

By the time Marcus could make an effort to stop what was going on, Nikki had been used for as much as the figure wanted from her. Marcus had been defeated by something more violent than the wind, and yet just as invisible. Only the effects were unmistakably apparent. He had failed her again...

With tears flowing from his eyes, and his legs almost too weak to carry him, Marcus made his way to Nikki. Her eyes opened to greet him, and the pleasure of the past few moments glowed at him.

"Oh, Marcus..You've never felt so good to me...I love you so much, honey.."

Fighting the increased flow of tears as much as he now fought the urge to go along with her for her benefit, he lost both battles.

"That wasn't me, Nikki...." He cried as he looked away from her face, too sick to look at her.

"Don't tease me, Marcus. Of course it was you. You're here aren't you?"

The puzzlement in her voice made him feel a little better. But she had been violated by some....some thing. He could only take so much of this before he had the breakdown he had feared for weeks.

"It wasn't meee..." He whined as the tears made a spot on the turned back sheet. "It was.....It was that thing..I couldn't stop it. It had me all over the house and everywhere else........I couldn't stop it!!"

And then he totally fell apart. He wrapped

himself around her, and as the shock of the moment
hit her, she also began to cry.

They had both been so helpless and unprepared,
and now the whole world crashed down on them.
Whether their marriage could survive the attack
didn't occur to them. For the moment, only pain
and degradation flowed from their eyes.

CHAPTER 11

With only two weeks of school left, Eric knew
he shouldn't be at home, sick and about to throw
his guts up. The last weeks of school were
considered the most important part of the year.
What it came down to though was FEAR, total and as
absolute as any eleven year old could ever know.
He could not leave the house. The mere thought of
leaving the house and going to school made his
stomach churn. Under these circumstances, he
really seemed sick to the rest of his family, and
they even felt sorry for him. If they could have
known the real reason for his condition, they would
be as terrified as he was. The nightmares had
rolled through his sleep since he'd seen the thing
on the corner. The funeral home had come up in
them every time, and in the past few, a strange
man. The man seemed familiar, but he couldn't
place him.

Under these conditions, the time crept by with
every sudden movement material for his imagination.
The thing would come for him again. If he had been
important enough to watch the day before, he didn't
have much time left now. It had to be waiting for
him to leave his house. His only alternative, he
couldn't leave. Now, or ever!

A phone call that evening changed everything.
A scream outside his room broadcasted the call, and
nearly sent him through the roof. His little
sister had a daily habit of doing that, but
everything was getting to him now. The phone call
itself really threw him for a loop. He could
hardly believe it was Pete.

"Eric..." The whispered voice asked as he

picked up the phone. The weakness of it surprised
Eric. It had to be Pete though, because it sure
sounded like him.

"Where are you, Pete? Where have you been?"

"I have to talk to you Eric. It's important."

"Sure, Pete, but where are you? I'm sick
right now, so I can't leave the house. Can you
come over here?"

The hesitation in Pete's voice gave Eric his
answer. Something had to be wrong.

"No...I can't. Can you meet me behind the
funeral home? It's important..."

"Well...uh..I guess, Pete. Give me some time
though, O.K.?"

The phone went dead. Eric felt an intense
dread sweep over his body. He didn't want to leave
his house, but now he had to. Pete could be hurt,
or even worse. He had to brave the figure's threat
and get to Pete somehow.

The idea of protection had to be considered.
Would it be smart to call the police and tell them
where Pete would be meeting him? If the cops were
there, he'd feel a lot better. Pete might hate him
for it, but he didn't want to die trying to help
his friend. That'd be really stupid.

Before he even attempted to leave his house,
he gave the police a call. An SNIU agent answered,
and seemed to appreciate the information more than
Eric appreciated a good baseball game. They'd be
there for him. They made that absolutely clear.
He felt a little safer now. He only had to force
himself out of his house.

As Janet lay in bed wondering what Norman was
doing, the insanity of her previous night slowly
crept into her consciousness. She had enjoyed the
party a little too much, and had stumbled out to
her car sometime after midnight, alone and in need
of some male companionship. Norman would be
waiting for her, but he would be tired and pissed
off at her because she was wasted. He hadn't
really wanted her to go in the first place, and she
would probably pay for her little bout of freedom
when she made it to his house. Not a very
promising thought.

Fumbling to get her key in the car door, a man came up from behind and nearly scared the fluids right out of her body. She hadn't caught his name, but he asked her for a ride home since his friends had left without him.

He seemed promising at the time, so she climbed into her car, sliding midway over in the seat to allow him to drive. Seconds later, they were heading along the road to who knows where.

Unable to control herself, she slid her hand between his legs as he drove, and began to divert his attention from the road. The next thing she knew, they were pulling down the first dark side road they came across. Moments later, she realized they were at the old funeral home!

With inhibitions totally out the window, they pulled their clothes off and fell to the ground at the funeral home back door. The ground was soft, and they rolled around for a long time before they heard a scream coming from inside the building.

The guy jumped up, threw some clothes on, and ran around the building looking for a way in. Scared, she felt safer with him, and followed after him to the side of the funeral home.

He crawled through a broken window and reached around to pull her in with him. She felt the cold sensation of moisture on her skin as the glass shards in the window sliced her legs. It didn't matter, she didn't feel any pain.

Once inside, they stumbled around until they made it through a doorway and out into a large open space. A small sound at the top of a large set of stairs beckoned them up, and they moved toward it. At the top, they found a small huddled mass, and realized it was human.

The sight nearly made her throw up. A pool of blood lay by his head, and streaked down from his mouth. He was dead, and already growing pale in the dim light of the old place.

Thumping sounds at the end of the hallway pulled their attention away from the disgusting sight at their feet, and they slowly moved toward them. Fear was taking the drunken haze from their thoughts, and they were beginning to realize the stupidity of what they were doing when a dark figure came towards them from down the hallway. She screamed and turned back towards the stairs, forgetting about the man with her. Before she knew it, she was back to her car, and frantically plowing down the driveway towards the main road.

She had left the man behind, but had forgotten about him until now!

The current horrors of her life flooded back to her. She had been tasked with going back to the old funeral home, had lost the boyfriend that at one time meant so much to her, and now remembered having left a man to die. The whole nightmare had fallen on her in the past few days, and she was still reeling from it.

Looking for the thousandth time at the strange old papers from the mail, Janet couldn't understand the meaning of the final sentence: "Go to the walled basement".

It just didn't make sense. What basement? There hadn't been a reference to a basement before that. He had to have made a mistake. Then again, sanity wasn't a bright spot in old Eagan's life from what she knew.

An image of the old funeral home floated into her mind. With another glance at the eerie black and white photograph from the package, the funeral home itself pulled her attention away from the central figure. The darkened windows of the two floors reached nearly from floor to ceiling in the rooms she had been in, even though the ceilings were extremely high. There weren't any lower windows indicating a basement. The picture just didn't give proof of a basement, or at least not by the presence of a window. In fact, Norman hadn't shown a basement to any of the prospective buyers when she had been around. Not that it meant there wasn't one, but it seemed unlikely to her. Norman would have at least mentioned it once in passing in all of the time she spent with him. He loathed that place, and it was constantly a topic of conversation.

She fought the urge to call him. He wouldn't talk to her. He hadn't the last fifty times she had gotten through to him, and a question about the funeral home wouldn't exactly break through the wall he had built between them. She had never seen stairs to a basement anyway. The only way she would know for sure though would be to find out for herself. It would mean going back to the funeral home, and the stupidity of the thought made her heart sink.

Whether as a result of wild imaginations sparked by the movies, or actual occurrences, strange phenomena dotted the pages of the paper occasionally, and filtered about the town by word of mouth as well. Since she had arrived here, a week hadn't passed without her hearing a ghost story. It sent chills down her spine. It also brought a remembrance of all the people who told her to never go into the funeral home. Those words still hung in her mind, and had kept her away from the place when she was younger and apparently wiser. But there had always been a small part of her that wanted to go in there for some stupid reason.

The idea that she would be able to stop some evil spirits seemed very unlikely to Janet. The manuscript didn't even outline a procedure. Hours of thought on the matter had only managed to complicate what little was in the pages, and then a real problem still lay at the base of the matter; on one side of the coin, the world, and on the other, her life. She had come to that conclusion within twenty minutes, and it seemed a realistic enough interpretation.

How could she compare her one life to the lives of the rest of the people in the world? They far outweighed her own meager existence. She was scared though, mostly for her own life but also because she might fail. It had to be done... What did she really have to live for besides her son anyway? Definitely not Norman! In reality, he hadn't been worth much in the first place. She had come to realize that it was the excitement of the conquest that had driven her more than his incessant sweet talk. What a revelation! To think she had figured it all out in three miserable days without the help of a shrink or even a priest.

The thought of bringing a priest or some other cleric into what she had to do passed in and out of her mind quickly, and happened to be the last thought she had before she walked out the door. The click of the lock behind her sealed it from being more than just a thought. Parchment in hand, the short walk to her car passed far too quickly for her. The emotional strain caused by simply pulling her car onto the street almost changed her mind.

After driving through town, she pulled onto Restview Way, not more than a mile from the funeral home. Second thoughts continued to plague her. It really pissed her off that her crazy uncle had pushed this off on her. Sure, he was her distant relative, but where did he get off sending this horrible nightmare her way. Hell was a good place for him as far as she was concerned. Whether he currently dwelt there or not, she definitely didn't want know.

In the haze of these thoughts, her car swerved slightly to the side of the road, and only the raised curb kept her from hitting a tree or whatever else might have gotten in the way. At the same time, she came to the edge of the funeral home's massive lawn. The flash of what seemed like a hundred police car lights drew her attention to the funeral home. They lit the entire area, and distracted her long enough to not see the little kid who had just maneuvered his bike into the path of her car. A dull thump on the car's right side brought Janet's foot to her brake pedal, and she screeched to a stop. But the boy lay on the road already, twisted among his bike frame.

All thoughts of her task flew from her mind. She had come to end some long festering problem, and now she had ended a kid's life instead. When would all of this nightmarish crap end?

Frantically stumbling out of her car and getting to the boy as quickly as possible, she soon found herself surrounded by policemen, men in suits, and what had to be soldiers.

"What happened here, lady?" A uniformed man asked as another ran off to his car to radio for an ambulance.

"I....I don't know.. He just came out of nowhere." She said desperately. It was the only

174

thing in her mind now, and it wasn't a better replacement for what she had already been thinking.

The boy looked just like her son had a decade before. Tears flooded her eyes and turned every flashing light into a star. Barely able to see, she stumbled back around her car and crawled hopelessly into her back seat. She might need to lie down. It was a good thing she hadn't eaten much that day.

Although it definitely wasn't on her mind, she soon had the cause of the huge convergence of authorities on the funeral home. It was a manhunt for two missing boys. They had been gone for days and she didn't know a thing about it. Pretty pathetic in a town of three thousand, she thought as she kicked herself over and over for being here. Swallowing hard, she wiped the tears from her eyes and looked around for the first time. She had never seen so many uniformed people in one place in Hawthorne. This many uniforms couldn't have even come from a fifty-mile radius in this area. The soldiers stood out in particular, and it was the soldiers that brought her some relief. Then the sight of Eric's eyes as they snapped open with the aid of smelling salts gave her the most relieved moment of her life. The boy would probably be O.K. But the missing boys still hadn't been found, and these people were about to tear the old funeral home apart to get to the bottom of the bike boy's story.

As Janet sat back in her car to collect her thoughts, she realized that her prospects were actually better now than they had been when she left her house. The policemen and soldiers were definitely the answer. They would buffer any danger she was waltzing into if she could even get into the place now.

Glancing around the crowd, she recognized two policemen she had talked to the night of the party. It was a long shot, but if she told them she was familiar with the layout of the old place, they might let her go along on the search. It was hopeless…well, hopeless and crazy, but she had to give it a try. Hitting the kid had, for some reason, solidified her resolve. Nothing to lose….

175

nothing to lose… played through her mind like a
restless tune making her just as restless. Pulling
herself together, she approached one of the
officers she recognized among the crowd, and was
soon talking to an SNIU agent and a uniformed woman
who appeared to be taking command of the entire
operation. She learned through whispered talk that
the woman was General Cochise of the Apache
military and that she was also a high-ranking
politician in the Intertribal Council. Everyone
deferred to her and the local police could do
little more than stutter in her presence. Aside
from that, whether they needed to be or not, she
and her soldiers were armed to the teeth, and the
mere presence of so many guns was somehow
comforting. The arrival shortly afterwards of a
massive, street-filling Apache military command
center and even more soldiers strengthened the
resolve that had been building in her since hitting
the kid. It didn't matter now that she didn't know
what the hell she was doing; she had enough support
to brave a visit to her uncle in hell.

        Despair still rocked the Lemonte house. The
probing lights of the police cars surrounding the
funeral home barely penetrated the misery Marcus
and Nikki wallowed in. The hurt would be forever,
and if forever was anything like the past few
hours, it would be unbearable. The pounding at the
front door of the house went unheard for at least
ten minutes. But an acknowledgment that something
was going on at the funeral home eventually roused
Marcus due to the incessant banging at the front
door.
        "Honey....come with me. I can't leave you
alone again.." He whispered to her.
        But stepping away from the bed, Marcus saw the
total helplessness that had overcome Nikki. She
remained there, her face buried in the pillow,
shaking with the force of her sobs. He couldn't
leave her again. He would carry her downstairs to
the front door with him. He wouldn't allow another
trick to take her away from him. When he started
to pick her up, she didn't resist him as she
usually would have. With a suddenness that

startled him, she wrapped her arms around his neck and held him so tight that he could barely breathe. The steps went slowly, and the frenzied pounding continued. This had damn well better be important, Marcus thought as he reached for the doorknob.

As if being chased by demons, the figure flung itself into the house before the door even stood fully open. Not until he turned back around to face him did Marcus realize that the maniac at the door was Matt.

"What the hell do you want?" Marcus asked, already pointing to the door for him to leave.

"You..you just have to let me talk to Nikki..." Matt said heavily, trying to catch his breath.

"As you can see, you stupid shit, Nikki is in no condition to talk to you, and even if she was, she wouldn't. I wouldn't allow it!"

"No, you don't understand." He continued breathlessly.

"Damnit, I don't really care. Now get the hell out of my house!" Marcus screamed, his anger bringing the smell of hotdogs and popcorn briefly to him.

But Matt had gotten in, and that was where he planned to stay. He would have to do whatever it took to get Marcus to listen to him. Marcus did seem to be right about Nikki. She looked terrible, and so did Marcus as far as that went. But they had to listen to him.

With Nikki in his arms, Marcus could do nothing to stop Matt as he turned and walked straight into their living room and sat down on their couch. The man was unbalanced, Marcus thought. Couldn't he tell that he wasn't wanted here? Marcus shuffled slowly into the living room since by now he was struggling to hold Nikki up. He would have to use some psychology on this fruitcake. He was unhinged and there was no telling what he would do.

Taking a seat, but still holding Nikki in his arms, Marcus gave in.

"All right, Matt. What do you want?"

The moment of hesitation that followed seemed to swallow up the past few minutes and leave

nothing behind but a garbled blur. Finally, with
only a stare coming from Marcus's face, Matt let
out a great shuddering sigh and began.

"Do you believe in spirits? You know, ghosts
and demons and whatever else people consider
supernatural."

Matt's words unexpectedly hit home for Marcus.
The night's experience welled up in his mind like a
snake about to strike, and with it came the fear
and rage that he had felt before. Muscles tensing,
he sat more rigidly on the couch with his hated
smells beginning to erupt.

Deciding to go on without an answer, Matt
sensed the sudden return of tension across the
room. He was getting through. Marcus was actually
listening.

"I think that a demon killed by best friend."
He blurted abruptly.

"What the hell!" Marcus exclaimed, the
tension climbing exponentially.

"I felt it... It's been around me..and....it
killed my best friend.." He muttered.

These muttered words now struck Marcus
peculiarly. He hadn't heard anything about a death
in Hawthorne since Ray Krepp's. Matt had either
lost it or more likely was trying to scam him.

"What are you talking about?" He asked
suspiciously.

"Just this weekend, he died in the Patton
hospital..." Matt muttered further.

Again, the room became still except now the
phone was ringing and it seemed far away and in
some other house. It continued and Marcus finally
realized it was their phone. Still carrying Nikki
with him, he somehow managed to get up from the
couch and shuffle into the kitchen carrying the
smells with him.

"Is this Marcus Lemonte?" The person on the
other end of the line asked as he picked up the
phone.

"Yes, this is Dr. Lemonte." He replied
weakly. He had only answered the phone with a plan
to hang up immediately and kill the nonstop
ringing.

"This is the Shawnee Nation Investigative

Unit. We understand that you own the funeral home on Restview Way. Is this true?"

He recalled the flashing lights now, and the hesitation that followed in the conversation made the agent on the other end of the line uneasy

"Yes." Marcus said, waiting to hear the worst.

"Uhhh..doctor...if you haven't noticed out your windows, we're preparing a large-scale search over here. We'd like for you to come over if you could. We will pick you up if necessary."

Pausing again, Marcus finally said, "No, no..that's O.K. I'll come over there. What's this all about? I thought you had to have a search warrant before you could search a place. I mean, I don't really care, but what the hell's going on?"

"We had a tip that the two missing boys were holed up in the funeral home. It was too urgent for protocol. You can understand the circumstances, I'm sure."

Marcus paused again, but this time he heard the line go dead. It was more than he could handle tonight. For a second, he stood in the kitchen, forgetting that he had Nikki in his arms. Then the strong smell of hotdogs and popcorn returned in full force along with the feeling he was being watched. Marcus looked out the window and then into the living room. Matt must have been listening to his phone call because someone had definitely been staring at him. It wasn't just paranoia this time; it was intense and well defined. The room started to close in on him and he leaned against and slid down the wall, somehow keeping Nikki in his weakening arms. He just couldn't fit things together right now. A loud cough from the living room briefly caught his fading attention. Matt was in there, but he couldn't make it back. His attention lapsed completely, the dreaded smell became overwhelming, and he blacked out.

At the same instant in the living room, Matt's mouth twitched in anxiety. His tension and fear were again building, and he could now also feel an ungodly presence forcing its way into his perception. In desperation, he wished that it

179

would end. But it continued, overwhelming him with terror. And then the figure from his dreams appeared! The dark figure from the corner! It now stood in the doorway to the living room, and began to gradually approach him, its shadowed face slowly becoming visible. A twisted, distorted mask appeared, and Matt realized the hideous smile was coming from Marcus's face. It hung before Matt shrouded in blackness. Tears came to his eyes as utter hopelessness swallowed him. Frozen in place, he could do nothing but stare. Suddenly, a massive rush of force swept over him, instantly crushing and shredding him to pieces before he could utter a cry or think of moving.

Janet pled her hopeless case for entering the funeral home aggressively, and the General stared at her without a word. After a few minutes of consideration, the General unexpectedly gave approval and walked off towards her command center. Janet stared after her briefly in shock and disbelief, but was then escorted to the front door of the funeral home to wait for the General's O.K. to enter. It took a little while, but Janet's resolve remained firm.

When finally ready and with the funeral home lit brighter than a baseball stadium, the General authorized her soldiers to enter through the front door and they did so with military precision. Janet, trying desperately to keep up with the pack, soon found herself at the base of the massive staircase staring at a pool of dried blood on the floor. An image of the man she had picked up at the party flooded her thoughts for a moment until she was pushed aside by two Apache soldiers on their way up. Janet panicked, the man might still be up there, DEAD!

"Hey, uhh... you'd better let me go up first," She muttered quickly, "we need to miss the rotten steps." She then managed to spit out, hoping they would buy her ridiculous line without question.

Amazingly, the soldiers stopping in mid-step and dropped behind her without a word, the General had sent Janet in with them because she knew the place. The woman had to be crazy or stupid, maybe

even both. It didn't matter, as long as they all
made it back out alive.

        Irrationally thinking that things were still
going in her favor, Janet grabbing the opportunity
before either she or the soldiers had more time to
think about it. Pretending to acknowledge the
presence of the imaginary danger, she climbed the
stairs, skipping a couple of steps near the top on
impulse. Ignoring the soldiers tailing her, she
moved rapidly down the hall after reaching the
second floor. If the guy from the party was dead
up there she thought, she had to be the first one
to get to him. It wasn't rational, but it seemed
strangely urgent all the same. When she reached
the first door, she paused for a moment to look
farther down the hall. The soldiers behind her
were seriously taping off the top steps before they
went on. Turning back the other way, she saw that
the hall was empty as far down as she could see.
If the guy had been attacked, he must have crawled
into a room or something. Of course, he could have
gotten out, but she hadn't heard anything about him
on the news or seen him around. She wasn't a big
fan of the local news and she had barely left her
house since that night, so it was a pretty
meaningless thought. Without thinking now, she
pulled the first door open only to find the stupid
closet behind it was completely empty as far as she
could tell and she quickly moved on. The next door
down the hall opened to another closet, hardly
worth the tension that was building as she moved
along. Her second wasteful delay had given two
soldiers time to make it over and stand directly
behind her. Looking past her and blocking her from
traveling further down the hall, one of the
soldiers flashed a light quickly through the small
doorway. Impatient and irritated by the
confinement, she followed the light around the
closet interior and caught sight of a dull dark
patch on the floor that she hadn't noticed in the
half-light. Stooping down to examine the closet
floor, one of the soldiers stumbled over her foot
as she tried to back out of her trap. A second
later he was gone, leaving both Janet and the other
soldier staring in disbelief. The only indications

the soldier had been there were a few scratch marks
through the dark residue covering most of the floor
in the closet. Janet blinked hard several times to
try to bring him back and immediately decided she
was losing it.

The other soldier recovered instantly calling
for assistance as he looked back to the stairs.
The soldier stayed at Janet's side as horrible
thoughts passed through her head. What the hell
had just happened? Her resolve wavered for a
second, but then a swarm of soldiers flew up the
stairs skipping the marked last two and surrounded
the closet door. The soldier who had called for
help used the barrel of his weapon to probe the
closet floor revealing a flap that gave with very
little effort, popping back up like it was spring
loaded. A trap door, they had found a trap door!

Before anyone could grab her, Janet stuck her
foot on the panel and it swung down with her
weight. Off balance, she fell through the hole,
and was out of sight before the soldiers knew it.

The sensation of falling swept over Janet and
all she could think was this was it...she was going
to die like a crazy idiot...... But the short fall
ended with a soft landing, or at least, soft for
her. It was too dark for her to tell, but it felt
like she had landed on another person. Whatever it
was, it had probably saved her pathetic life. A
sudden burst of light from the trap door thirty
feet above brought the whole morbid scene to her
horrified eyes. The twisted body of the vanished
soldier lay beneath her, along with several other
bodies in a rotten stinking mass of flesh. She
threw up before she could get off of the pile, the
bile filling her nose and adding to the stench.
Still choking as she moved, she watched as several
soldiers scurried down the ladder bolted to the far
side of the shaft she had just plunged through.
She had been extraordinarily lucky to miss it. The
dead soldier hadn't been as fortunate, and by the
looks of it, neither had a few others. The room
began to fill with soldiers, most trying
desperately to miss the disgusting pile of rotting
humans lying in their paths at the base of the
ladder. The most discernible figures in the pile

were those of two small boys, both bloating and
nearly unrecognizable. The soldier still lay on
top of them and would have survived the fall if it
hadn't been for the ladder. It was the obvious
explanation for the fact that his head had almost
broken clear of his spine. She shuddered and
thought at least it had been a quick death. It was
impossible to even guess how long the others in the
pile had suffered after the drop.

She shuddered again and then began to scan the
room to avoid looking at the rotting mess. A wall
of red brick caught her attention at one end of the
room, standing out from the rest of the walls that
had been made entirely of grey cement blocks.
Jumping to her feet, she swallowed back a gush of
bile, and crossed the room to the wall. This had
to be the place her old uncle was leading her to,
nothing else she had seen in the funeral home came
close to matching the translations on the old
parchment.

Leaning against the brick and deciding a
sledgehammer would be helpful, a loud click filled
the room and was followed by the unmistakable sound
of stone grinding on stone. She had tripped a
switch somewhere on the wall and the entire wall
began to swing open. The foul odor that poured out
through the gradually widening crack took her
breath away before she could stop inhaling. It was
all she could do now to keep the bile down. The
room full of soldiers stared at the opening that
had been a brick wall a moment earlier, none of
them making a move to stop Janet as she stumbled
into the adjoining chamber choking up bile. With
all of them now gasping for breath, the cave beyond
held their attentions like deer frozen in the
headlights of an approaching car. Only a couple of
them lost their stomach contents as the combining
stench permeated the stale air.

CHAPTER 12
Floating over the bloody, nearly decapitated
form that had recently been Matt, the dark figure

183

shifted to face the two propped against the wall down the short hallway. Marcus remained still and unconscious, now in an outwardly peaceful state that masked the status epilepticus storming his brain for the first time since hospitalized following his accident. Marcus's seizure drew the figure in toward him and it continued to drive the dark form into a frenzied rage as his seizures had ever since it had been pulled from the spirit world. Sweeping ragefully down the hall, it collected Nikki into its darkness, and abruptly vanished, appearing simultaneously in the funeral home basement with Nikki suspended below its hideously smiling face. The abrupt appearance of the figure in the already crowded basement pushed the soldiers into a chaotic frenzy. A scream expelled in terror was instantly muffled when the figure expelled a massive force that crushed the soldier's chest. With the collapse of the mangled soldier, the screams multiplied, becoming a deafening roar echoing into the small cave from behind Janet. The roar magnified the feeling of doom that nearly overwhelmed her as soon as she entered the cave. Even then, she clearly saw petroglyphs covering the walls of the cave before she was pushed deeper in as it quickly filled with desperately screaming soldiers and the mingled stench that swept in with them. Caught in the flow, she soon found herself plastered into a back corner unable to move more that a few inches.

With there expectations of compliance in the Shawnee Nation extremely low, even from a doctor, two SNIU agents had immediately driven the short distance to the Lemonte house to collect Marcus. Getting no response at the front door, one had walked around to peer through the back door glass into the kitchen. He gaped in shock as a dark mass swarmed over a man and woman propped against a wall on the kitchen floor. The darkness abruptly disappeared with the woman, leaving the man slumped over on the floor and possibly dead. Violently throwing the door open, the agent scrambled to Marcus in time to feel his thready pulse fade beyond perception.

Hearing the onset of ear busting screams over her headset, the General barreled out of the command center, weapon and her remaining soldiers in tow. She hit the ground running and was across the funeral home lawn before she had a chance to consider where she was going. SNIU agents and local police who had been content with the soldiers taking all the risk followed slowly behind the last soldier, weapons drawn, and the sweat of fear covering their faces. The screams could be heard from the road, and running toward them seemed wrong to anyone still able to think. The General didn't need to think. Her soldiers were in trouble and she had brought them here. Once inside, she followed the screams echoing down the massive staircase, and made it to the top only a little winded. Scrambling to the second closet door, she was the first down the trap door ladder in the closet. She jumped the last few feet to avoid the pile of bodies that had just been described over her headset. Counting three down already, she felt immediate guilt for being too late to save them. Unfortunately, the timing of her arrival was otherwise impeccable.

The instant Marcus's pulse faded with him into death, the dark figure was ripped through the back wall of the petroglyph covered cave, returning explosively to the spirit world it had escaped when Marcus died and was revived following his coma inducing accident. In the absence of total life support provided by an ICU, Marcus would not be returning to the living this time. As the figure disappeared through the cave wall, a careening soldier caught Nikki in mid air protecting her from the fall. A clap of thunder produced by the figure's return to the land of the dead blasted everyone in the cave and the attached room off their feet. They all remained on the ground for a while overwhelmed by the shock of the past few moments. Slowly, they realized it was over and their minds had already begun the struggle to barricade the event out of their memories to preserve their sanity. Even the open-minded soldiers with extensive spiritual beliefs would have trouble with this one. It was the making of nightmares and the future thief of sleep.

One of the last to stand up, Janet caught sight of the two mangled soldiers that had fallen to the figure. The General stood over them and Janet saw that her demeanor was no longer that of the woman in command she had pleaded to not long before. Regardless of everything else the General may have been, she continued to be human and she felt loss.

Janet staggered over to the only other civilian among the crowd. The soldier who had caught Nikki was then able to buffer her in the fall when they were knocked down by the concussive blast. She was now standing, but she appeared to be stunned or in some form of shock. Janet recognized the woman from the single visit she had made with her husband to Norman's realty office concerning the funeral home. There was a dramatic decline in her appearance, but it was Mrs. Lemonte. She felt pretty sure of it for some reason.

Gently grasping her arm, Janet tried to connect with Nikki. "Mrs. Lemonte…are you alright?" But the woman only stared at her without seeing. There was no point in pursuing her concern or trying to explain why she was here among this mess in the woman's funeral home. The woman wouldn't understand and probably wouldn't believe her if she did. If she had been alone to witness this and then tried to describe it to her own son, he would have had her locked away like her old uncle. The thought was vaguely comforting. Maybe her uncle hadn't been crazy after all.

Walking next to stand by the General, she observed the ragged mess the figure had made of the two soldiers. The General didn't move or acknowledge in any way that she was there, but it felt like the right thing to do and she stood there until the soldiers forced her to leave the Pit. Remarkably, someone had already given it that name, and it seemed more appropriate than anything else.

Back up the ladder, she was briefly blinded by an array of spotlights the SNIU had already carried up into the hallway. At least they could handle a

186

little manual labor. None of them had gone into
the Pit, and when none of them would even meet her
gaze, she realized they had no intention of ever
going down there. If she was being generous, she
could chalk it up to wisdom on their part, but they
didn't seem to deserve her generosity.

Again remembering the man she had left there
after the party, Janet made her way down the well-
lit hall. She came across a couple of pools of
dried blood, but the guy definitely wasn't in the
hall. Quick checks of the half dozen rooms on the
second floor revealed nothing, no more blood, and
no bodies. She felt a little relieved until she
imagined him being part of the mass of rotting
bodies in the Pit. That thought drove her out of
the funeral home and over to her car. She didn't
leave, she just felt better in something large,
solid and familiar.

CHAPTER 13

The following several weeks were spent trying
to explain the unexplainable both to herself and to
anyone else who would listen. The media was
unavoidable anyway, a whole train of vans having
reportedly followed the Apache mobile command
center to Hawthorne from some other local
investigation.

She also spent a fair amount of time talking
with the General who avoided the media like the
plague, but didn't seem to have any problems
talking to her. Maybe it had been the moments by
the General's side standing over her soldiers.
Maybe it was just witnessing the same bizarre
event. It didn't matter; Andrea seemed to benefit
from their talks as much as she did. She was the
most significant person who had ever given Janet
the time of day, but it seemed normal and it
bolstered the resolve that had driven her into the
Pit in the first place, and turned it into
something more significant.

Aside from the fact that the General and her
soldiers brought credibility to Janet's story and

kept her from following in her uncle's footsteps like she would have if she had been there alone, Andrea became her friend. A single event could do that sometimes, especially when death was involved. Death was the great equalizer of the world, no one could escape it.

The rediscovery of the Pit brought team after team of investigators to Hawthorne, and they all wanted first hand accounts from Janet, the only coherent civilian who witnessed the event in the cave, and the only person who was talking. It got old quickly, but there was talk of a book deal and she needed the money now that Norman was out of the picture. Work was a little scarce in Hawthorne. But she had grown up here and she couldn't imagine leaving.

When Mrs. Lemonte recovered from the shock and the additional loss of her husband, she wanted nothing more to do with the funeral home and didn't care if Janet took on the management of what developed. In fact, Nikki moved immediately out of her house next to the funeral home and only remained in Hawthorne due to the support of a friend who had also recently lost her husband. She now needed Hedda as much as Hedda needed her, and looking beyond their losses, they would soon have a baby to raise. Janet gradually befriended the two of them and kept Hedda apprised of findings at the Pit when Nikki wasn't around. Like Janet, Hedda had grown up in Hawthorne and her interest in the funeral home and what was below it was only natural.

In time, it came to be known that construction workers had apparently come across the buried cave during construction of the funeral home, and the owner of the land at the time, Pierre Lemonte, had greedily hoarded the find until his death, telling very few that the cave even existed.

The torrent of investigators drew quick conclusions based on previous findings throughout the broad expanse drained by the Mississippi River. The experts claimed the petroglyphs in the cave predated not only the Mississippian culture, but also the earlier Adena and Hopewell cultures. This would make them some of the oldest Native relics found and possibly remnants of the northern reaches of the Poverty Point culture that once inhabited land on the lower Mississippi. Some speculated that they were even relics of the first inhabitants of the continent dating back more than ten thousand years, but most of the experts were skeptical of this stretch.

Following a very brief assessment, the initial interpretation of the cave writings suggested the cave wall had been seen as a bridge to the spirit world by the extinct cultures that the Natives now called the Ancients. The disappearance of the dark spirit through the wall was black and white evidence of the validity of their beliefs to everyone who witnessed it. According to a reliable SNIU agent, what is assumed to have been the same figure had somehow transported Mrs. Lemonte out of her house next door, and per numerous eye witnesses, appeared in the cave with the woman out of nowhere. The last part can be viewed as a solid fact at this point. Further investigation of the cave and its contents would now proceed without the hindrance of the current property owner, the granddaughter-in-law of Pierre Lemonte, Nikki Lemonte.

In spite of the financial boon brought by researchers and investigative tourists, Hawthorne had suffered numerous losses all of which the authorities quickly blamed on the dark spirit. At least they desperately hoped the figure had been the culprit since any other explanation would leave a violent killer still roaming the town.

All together, seven Hawthorne residents died during the short time leading up to rediscovery of the Pit. The clothing store would remain open even though there were no known heirs to its owner. This was a unanimous and immediate town council decision. Hawthorne couldn't afford to let it close considering the number of people it brought in to town.

The loss of the town doctor would send people out of Hawthorne for their medical care. There was no alternative considering the difficulty of getting a doctor to permanently practice in such a small town.

The deaths of the two boys carried an unknown amount of damage to the town. They were still too young to contribute much to the community, but their loss was the loss of potential. Their friend Eric would suffer indefinitely from their deaths. He couldn't get beyond the fact that he had dared them to go to the funeral home in the first place, and the guilt was crippling.

The deaths of Ray and Phyllis were loosely attributed to the dark spirit based on reports of the deceased's spouses. But they still added to the population loss in a Nation that couldn't afford to lose anymore of its people, but would continue on regardless until there were none left.

THE END

ABOUT THE AUTHOR

The author currently lives with his wife and daughter in Las Vegas. He hasn't decided if there will be a Las Vegas in the Ravaging Myths world yet, but is open to suggestions.